Pinocchio

OM

Om Books International

Pinocchio

Om Books International

4379/4B, Prakash House, Ansari Road,
Daryaganj, New Delhi-110002
Tel : 91-11-23263363, 23265303   Fax : 91-11-23278091
E-mail : sales@ombooks.com   Website : www.ombooks.com
Copyright © 2009 **Om Books International**

First Published 2009

Text, Illustration & Design by Bookmatrix

ISBN : 978-81-87108-22-1

Printed in Singapore by:
Tien Wah Press (Pte) Ltd.

CARLO COLLODI

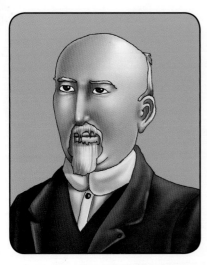

Carlo Collodi was an Italian author and journalist, best-known as the creator of Pinocchio, the wooden boy puppet who came to life. He was born on 24th November in 1826 as Carlo Lorenzini to Domenico Lorenzini, a cook, and Angela Orzali, a servant.

Carlo spent his childhood in the hillside village of Collodi with his nine siblings. After completing primary school, he went on to study for priesthood. However, after graduation he started working for a book seller and later plunged into politics. At the age of 22, he became a journalist and in 1848 founded the satirical journal 'It Lampione'. Meanwhile, Carlo also wrote comedies.

Later in his life, Carlo gave up journalism and turned to writing children's fantasies. He began translating the fairy tales of Charles Perrault. Afterwards, he wrote his own children's stories with a series called Giannettino.

Pinocchio first appeared in the Giornale Dei Bambini, a children's magazine in 1881 and was an immediate success. The story was of a wooden puppet who learned to be generous through hard lessons. As the story ends, Pinocchio ceases to be a Marionette and becomes a boy. The story of Pinocchio was translated into English in 1892 by M. A. Murray.

The story has inspired many film makers, including Walt Disney, whose animated film on Pinocchio was released in 1943. The story of Pinocchio speaks volumes about being truthful, unselfish and being brave.

Carlo Collodi died in Florence on October 26, 1890.

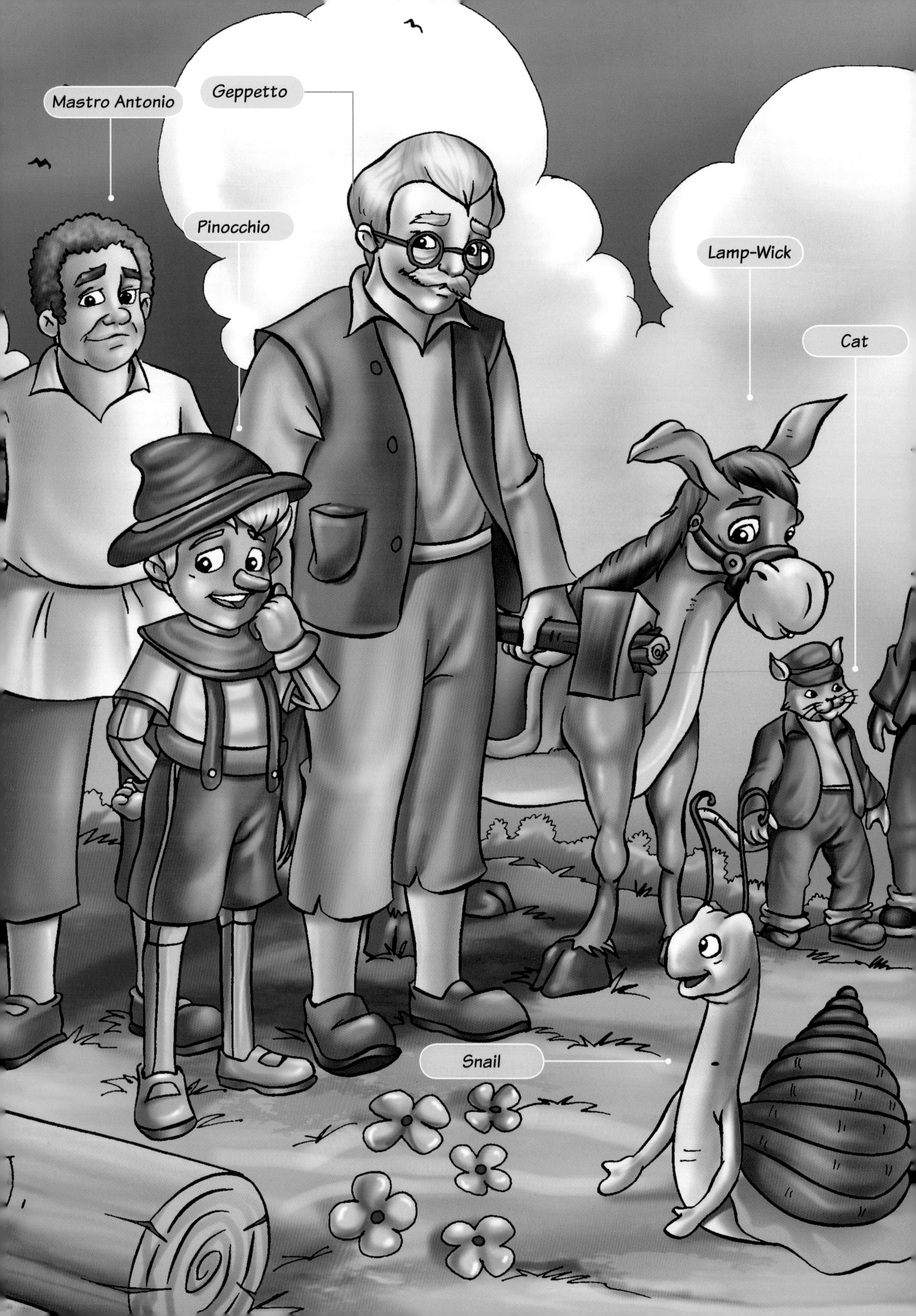
Mastro Antonio
Geppetto
Pinocchio
Lamp-Wick
Cat
Snail

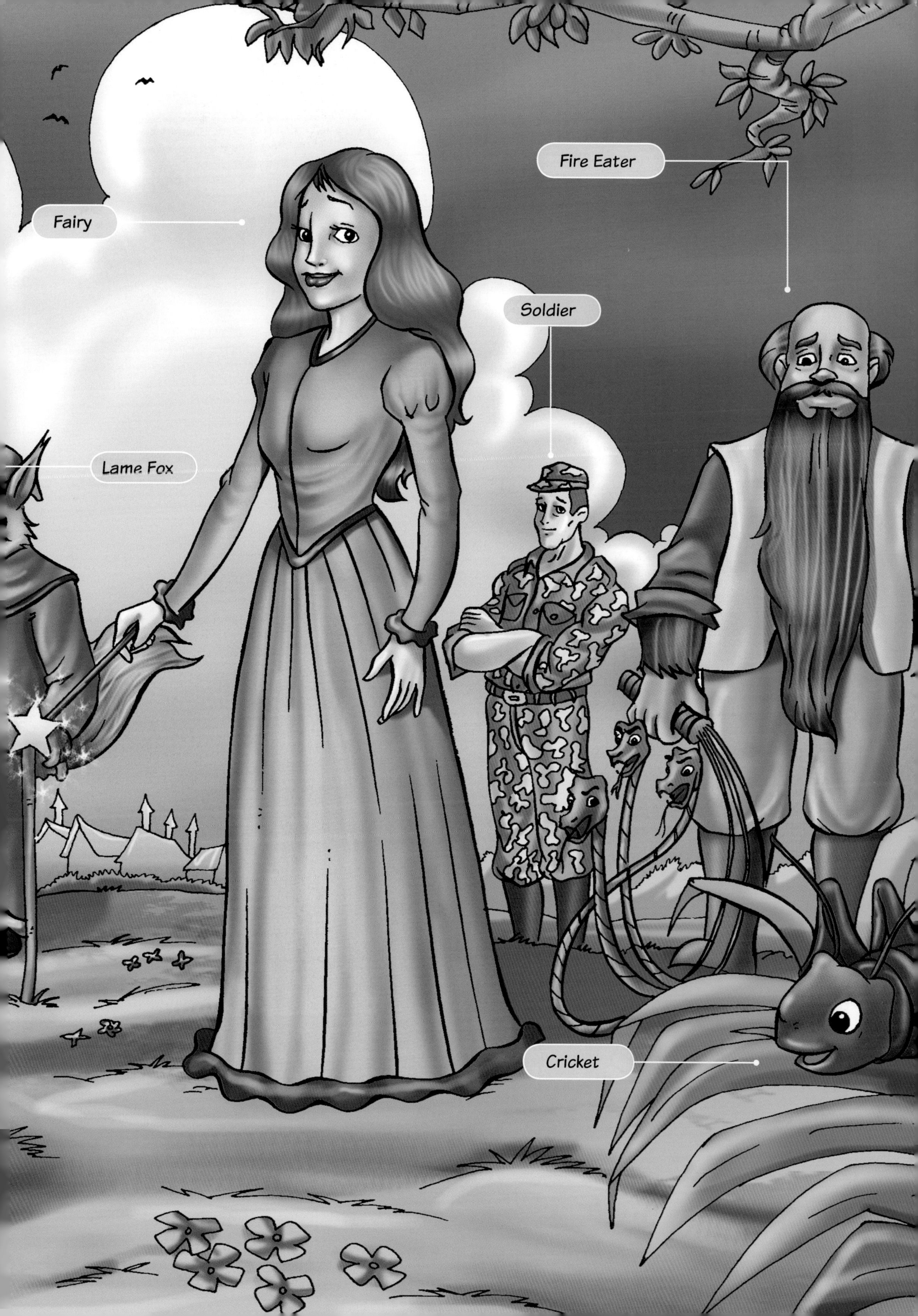
Fire Eater
Fairy
Soldier
Lame Fox
Cricket

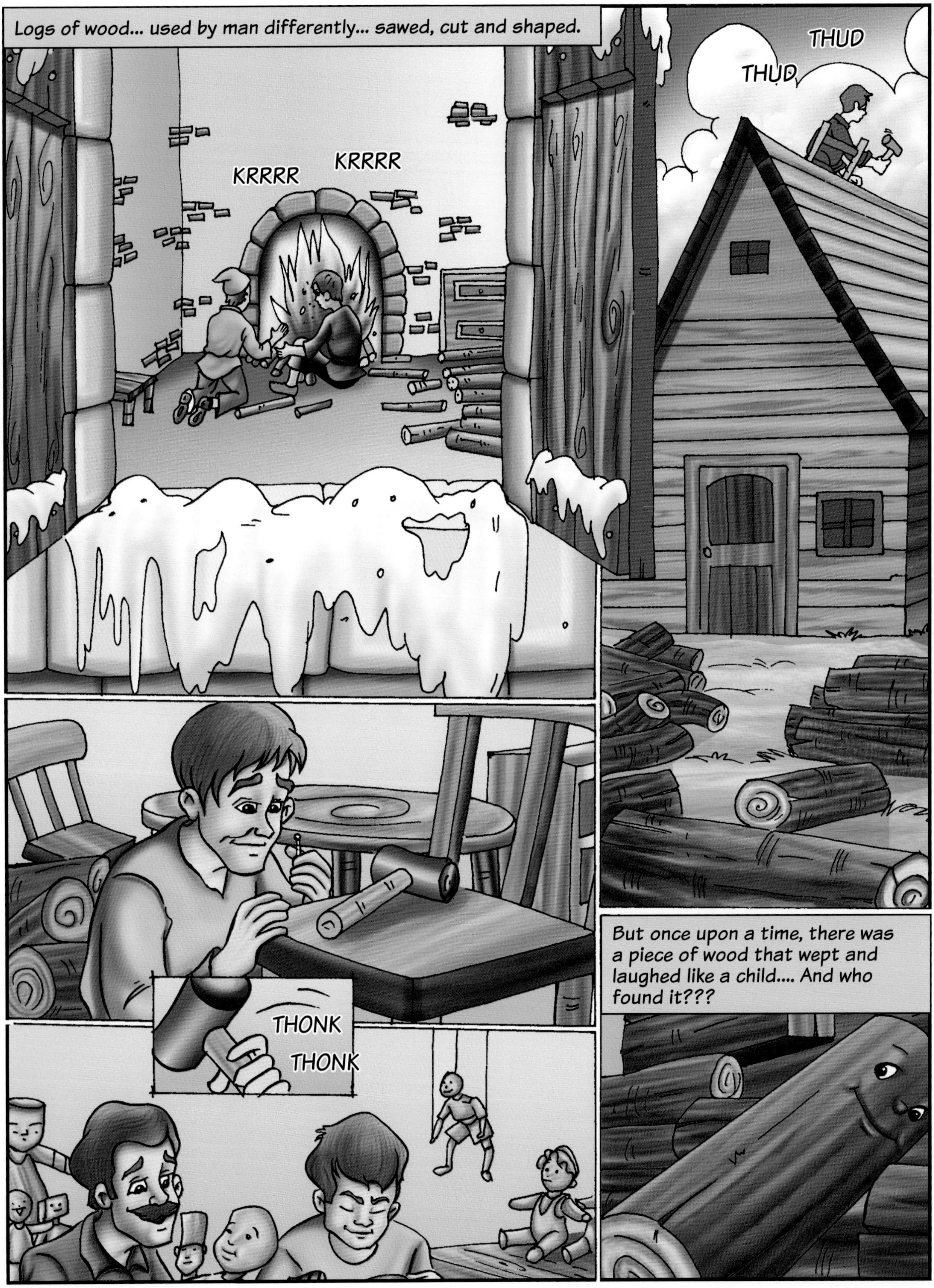
Logs of wood... used by man differently... sawed, cut and shaped.
KRRRR
KRRRR
THUD
THUD
THONK
THONK
But once upon a time, there was a piece of wood that wept and laughed like a child.... And who found it???

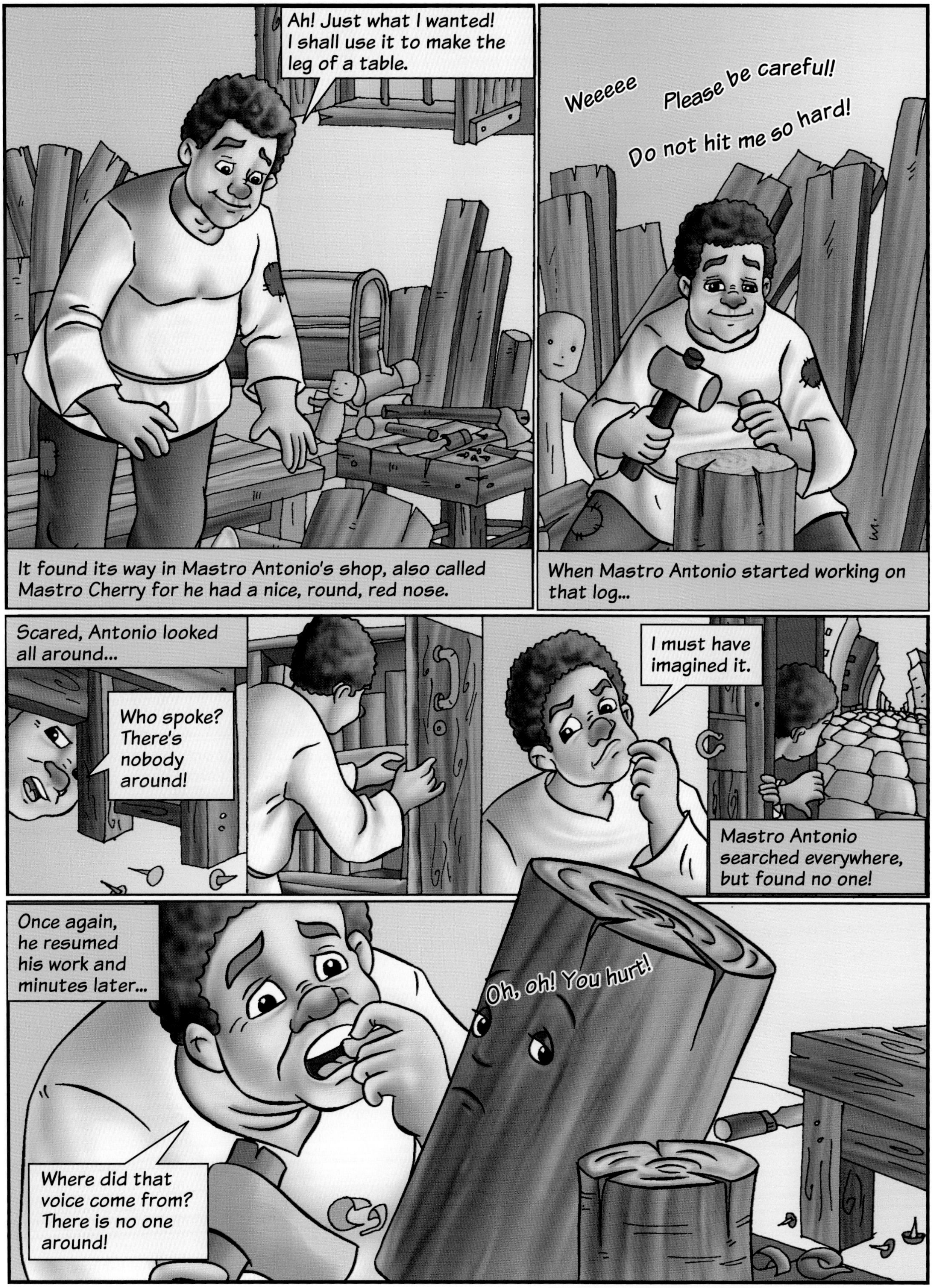
Ah! Just what I wanted! I shall use it to make the leg of a table.
It found its way in Mastro Antonio's shop, also called Mastro Cherry for he had a nice, round, red nose.
Weeeee
Please be careful!
Do not hit me so hard!
When Mastro Antonio started working on that log...
Scared, Antonio looked all around...
Who spoke? There's nobody around!
I must have imagined it.
Mastro Antonio searched everywhere, but found no one!
Once again, he resumed his work and minutes later...
Oh, oh! You hurt!
Where did that voice come from? There is no one around!

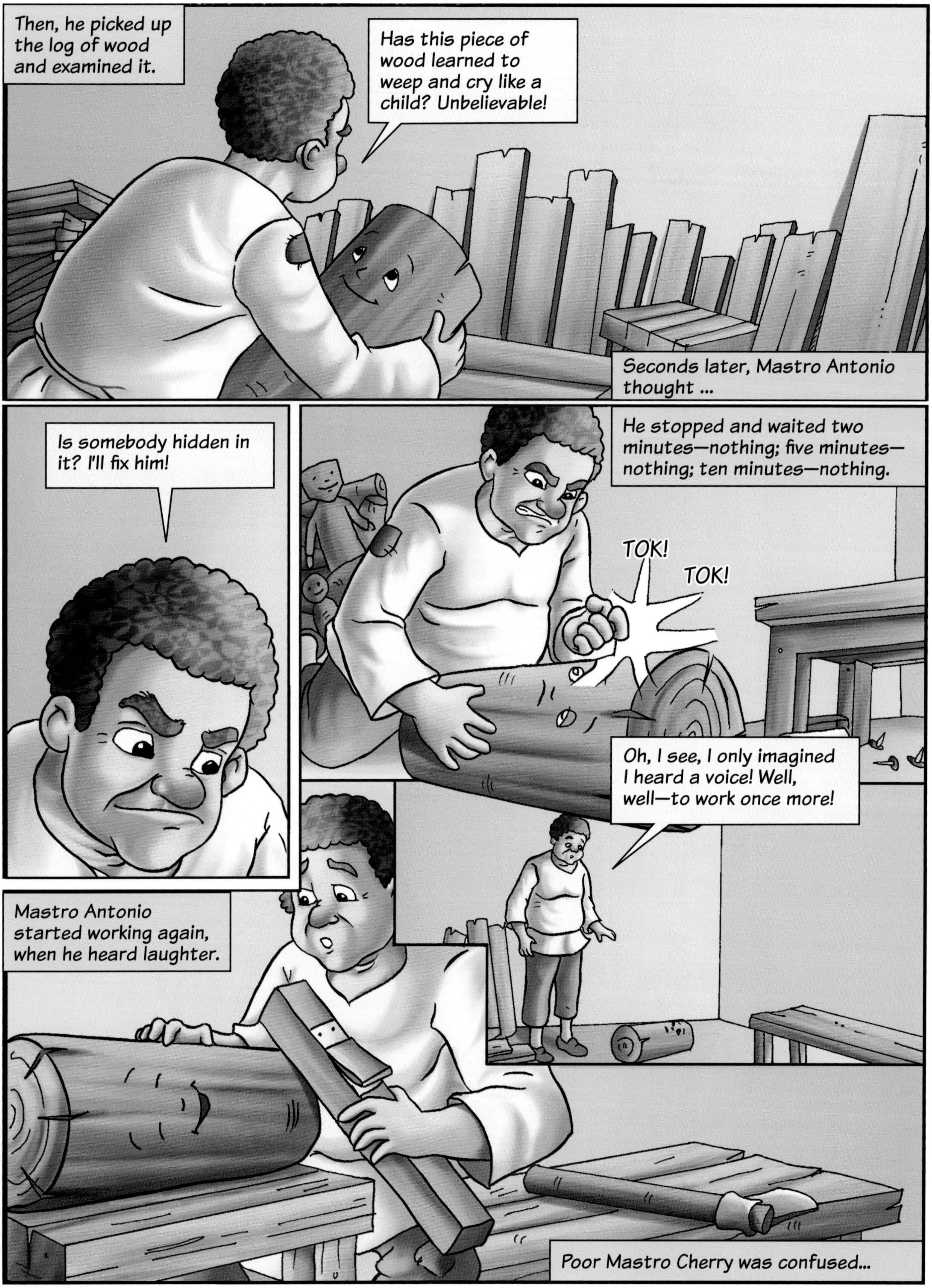
Then, he picked up the log of wood and examined it.
Has this piece of wood learned to weep and cry like a child? Unbelievable!
Seconds later, Mastro Antonio thought ...
Is somebody hidden in it? I'll fix him!
He stopped and waited two minutes—nothing; five minutes—nothing; ten minutes—nothing.
TOK!
TOK!
Oh, I see, I only imagined I heard a voice! Well, well—to work once more!
Mastro Antonio started working again, when he heard laughter.
Poor Mastro Cherry was confused...

Just then, there was a knock on the door.

KNOCK!

KNOCK!

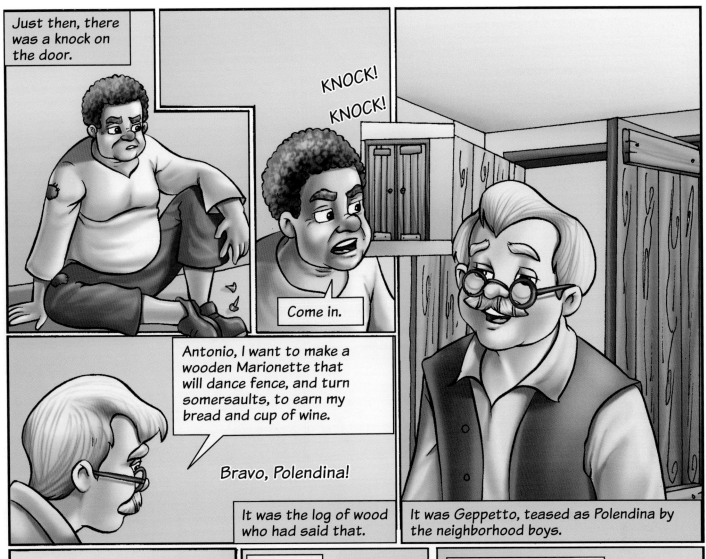

Come in.

Antonio, I want to make a wooden Marionette that will dance fence, and turn somersaults, to earn my bread and cup of wine.

Bravo, Polendina!

It was the log of wood who had said that.

It was Geppetto, teased as Polendina by the neighborhood boys.

Why do you insult me by calling me Polendina?

I did not.

They grew angrier with each passing minute. They went from words to blows and finally scratched, bit and slapped each other.

Give back my wig!

You return mine and we'll be friends.

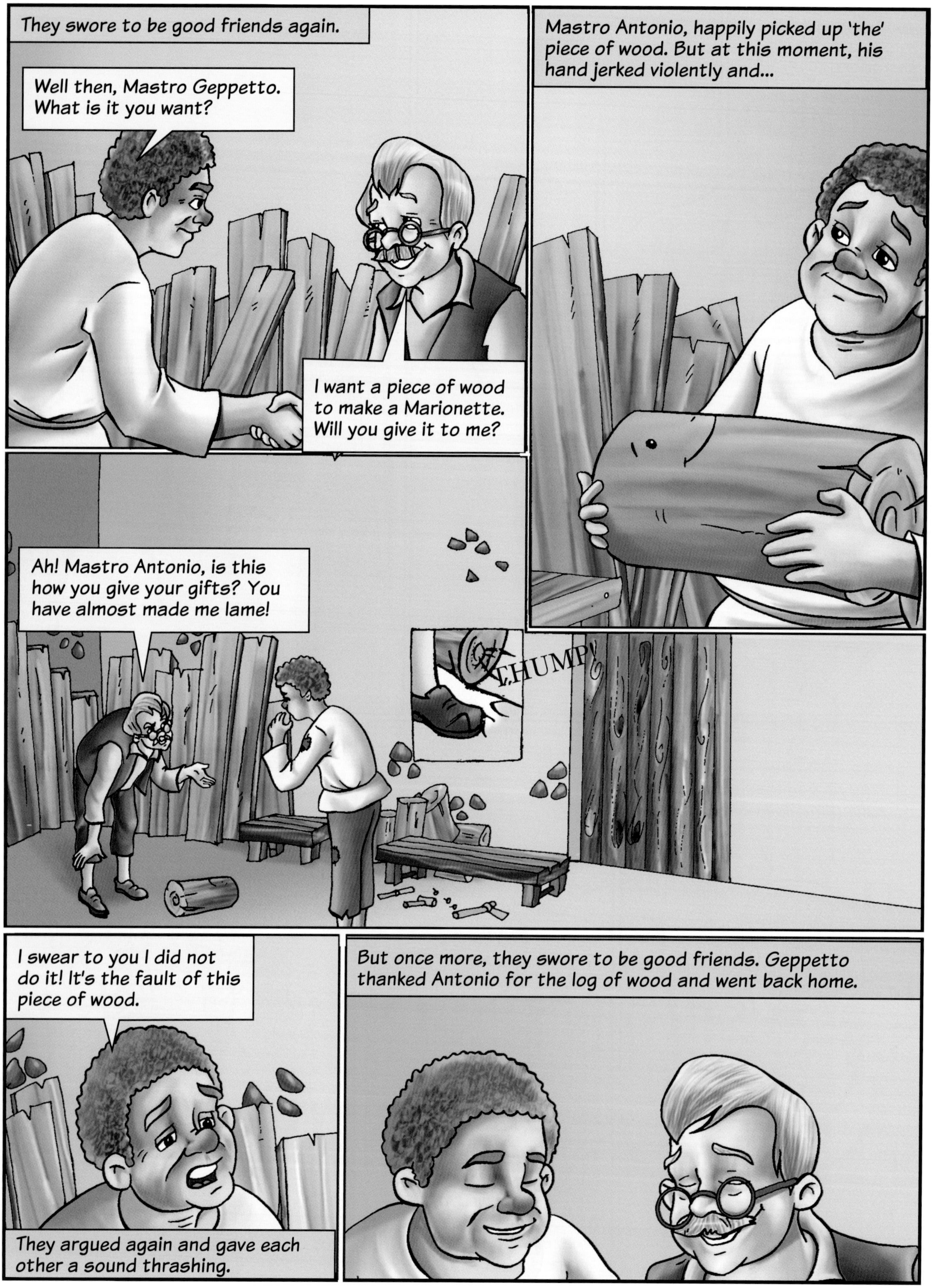
They swore to be good friends again.
Well then, Mastro Geppetto. What is it you want?
I want a piece of wood to make a Marionette. Will you give it to me?
Mastro Antonio, happily picked up 'the' piece of wood. But at this moment, his hand jerked violently and...
Ah! Mastro Antonio, is this how you give your gifts? You have almost made me lame!
THUMP!
I swear to you I did not do it! It's the fault of this piece of wood.
They argued again and gave each other a sound thrashing.
But once more, they swore to be good friends. Geppetto thanked Antonio for the log of wood and went back home.

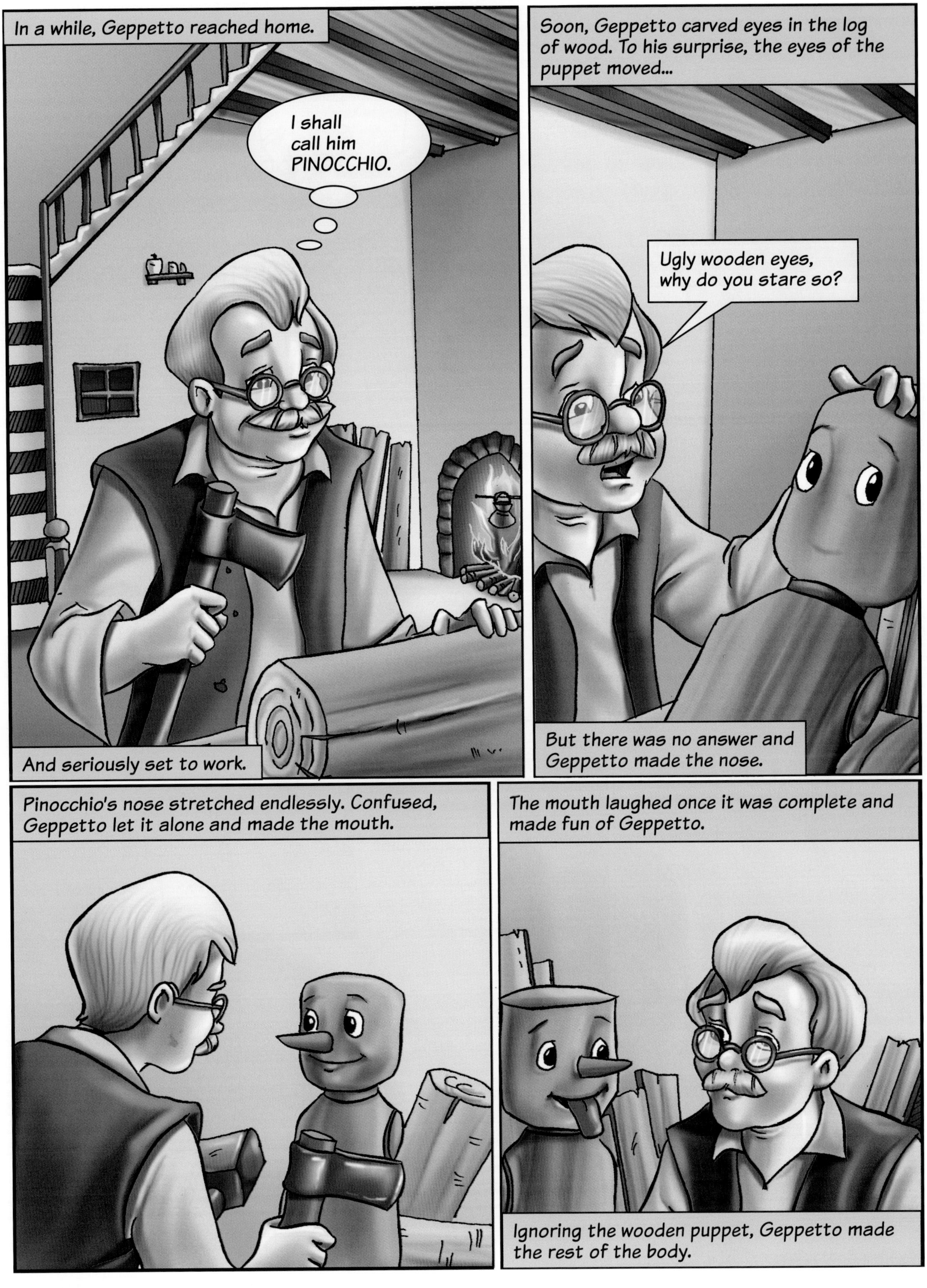
In a while, Geppetto reached home.
I shall call him PINOCCHIO.
And seriously set to work.
Soon, Geppetto carved eyes in the log of wood. To his surprise, the eyes of the puppet moved...
Ugly wooden eyes, why do you stare so?
But there was no answer and Geppetto made the nose.
Pinocchio's nose stretched endlessly. Confused, Geppetto let it alone and made the mouth.
The mouth laughed once it was complete and made fun of Geppetto.
Ignoring the wooden puppet, Geppetto made the rest of the body.

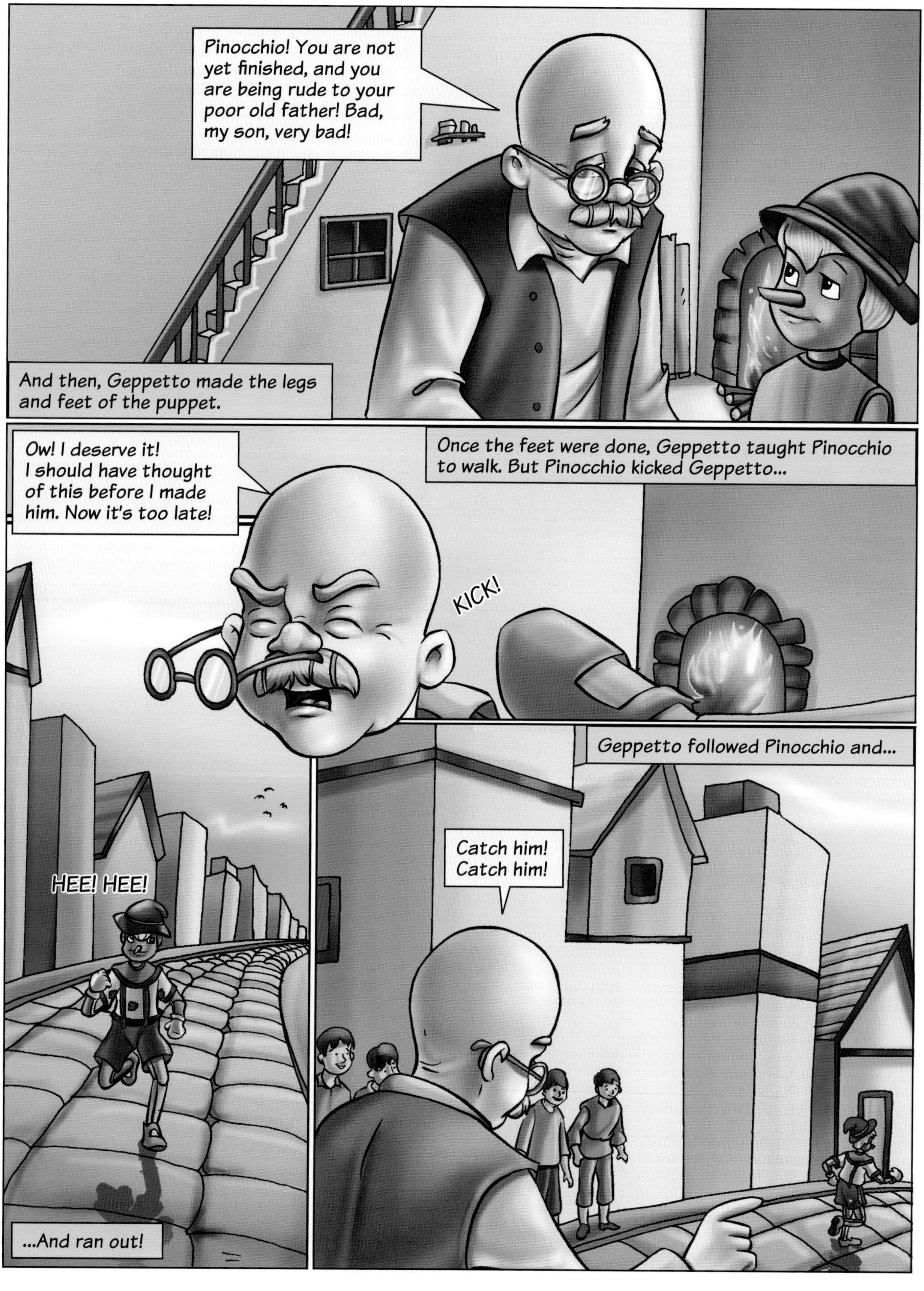
Pinocchio! You are not yet finished, and you are being rude to your poor old father! Bad, my son, very bad!
And then, Geppetto made the legs and feet of the puppet.
Once the feet were done, Geppetto taught Pinocchio to walk. But Pinocchio kicked Geppetto...
Ow! I deserve it! I should have thought of this before I made him. Now it's too late!
KICK!
HEE! HEE!
...And ran out!
Geppetto followed Pinocchio and...
Catch him! Catch him!

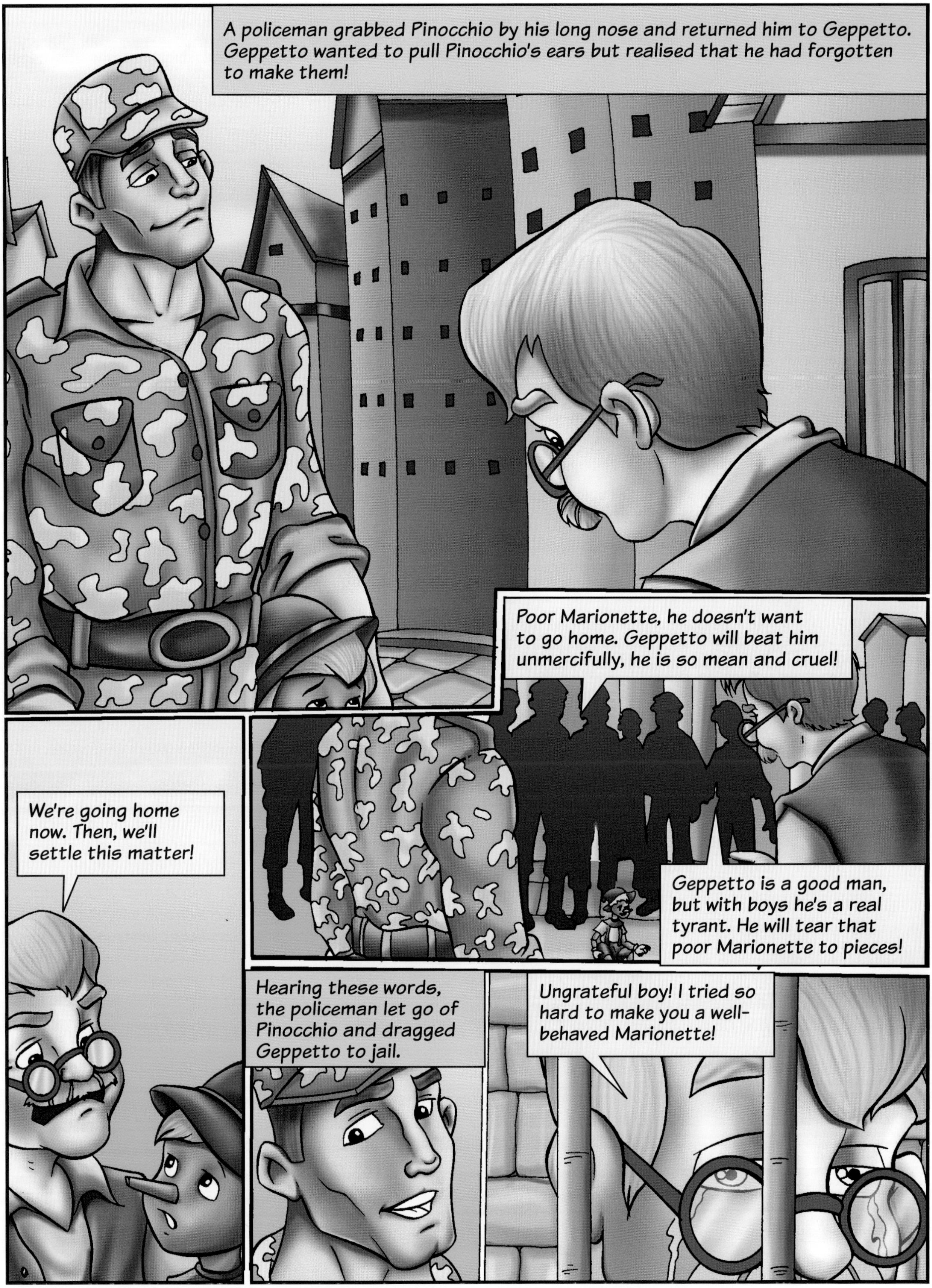
A policeman grabbed Pinocchio by his long nose and returned him to Geppetto. Geppetto wanted to pull Pinocchio's ears but realised that he had forgotten to make them!
Poor Marionette, he doesn't want to go home. Geppetto will beat him unmercifully, he is so mean and cruel!
We're going home now. Then, we'll settle this matter!
Geppetto is a good man, but with boys he's a real tyrant. He will tear that poor Marionette to pieces!
Hearing these words, the policeman let go of Pinocchio and dragged Geppetto to jail.
Ungrateful boy! I tried so hard to make you a well-behaved Marionette!

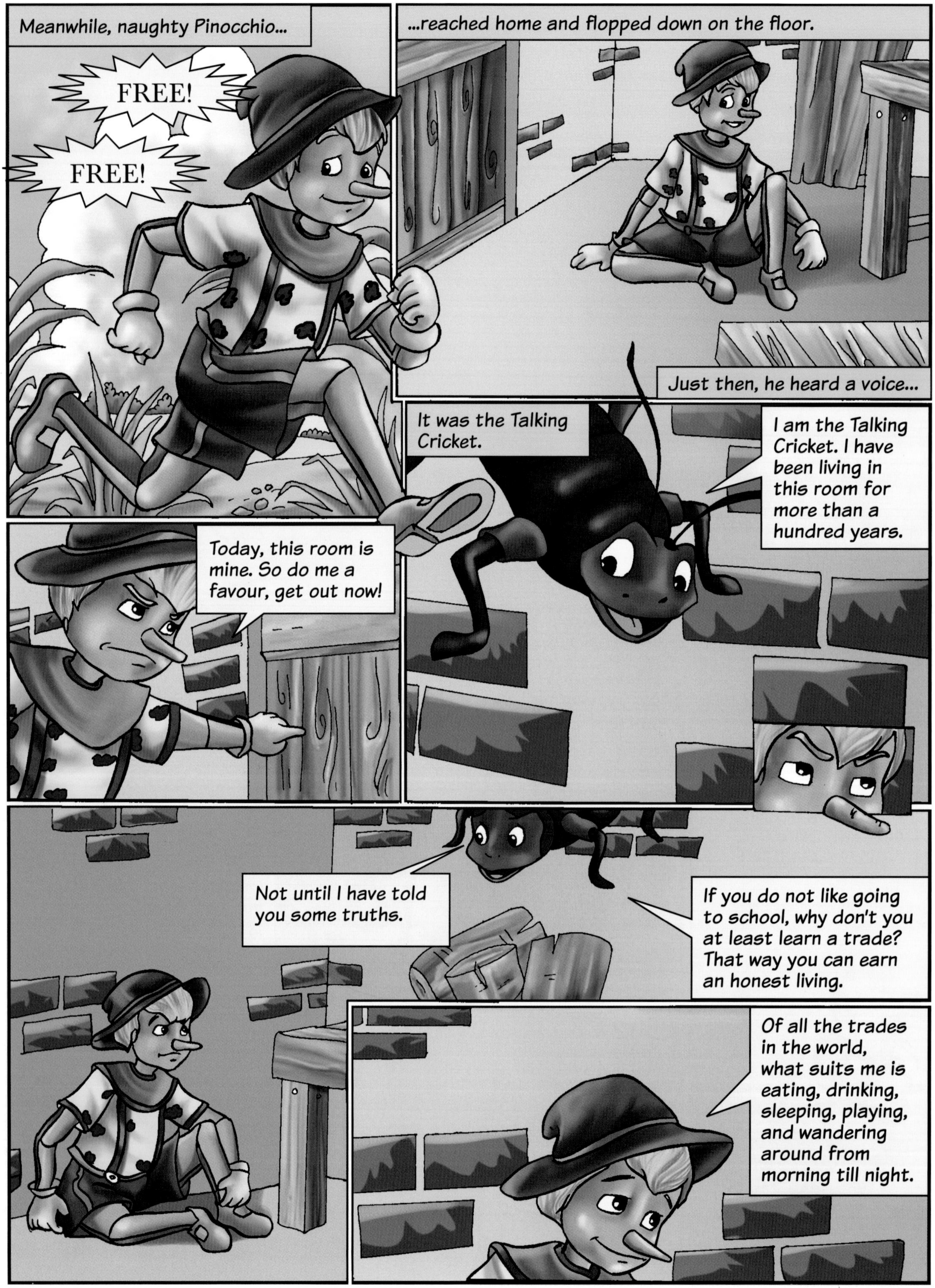
Meanwhile, naughty Pinocchio...
FREE!
FREE!
...reached home and flopped down on the floor.
Just then, he heard a voice...
It was the Talking Cricket.
I am the Talking Cricket. I have been living in this room for more than a hundred years.
Today, this room is mine. So do me a favour, get out now!
Not until I have told you some truths.
If you do not like going to school, why don't you at least learn a trade? That way you can earn an honest living.
Of all the trades in the world, what suits me is eating, drinking, sleeping, playing, and wandering around from morning till night.

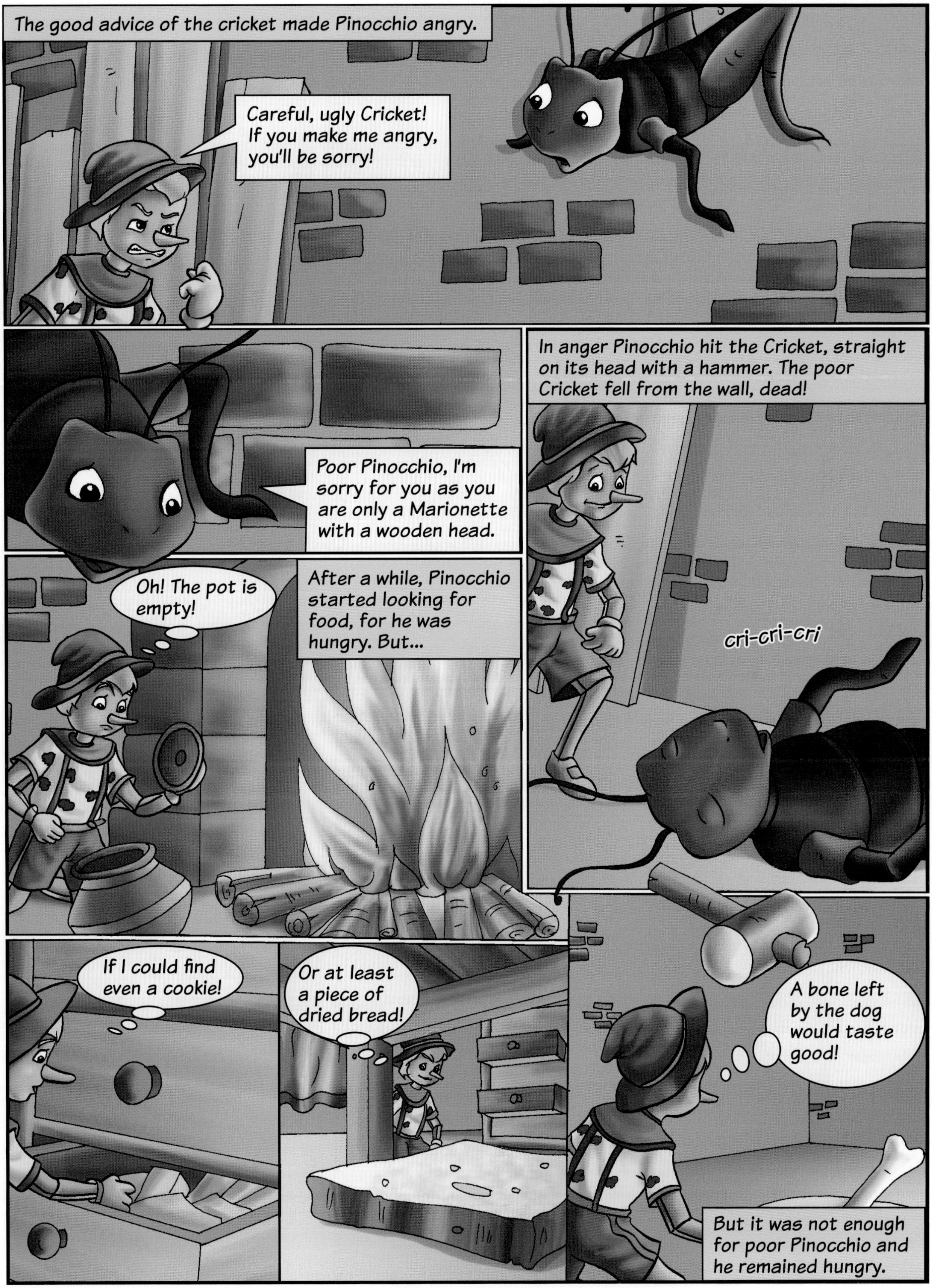
The good advice of the cricket made Pinocchio angry.
Careful, ugly Cricket! If you make me angry, you'll be sorry!
Poor Pinocchio, I'm sorry for you as you are only a Marionette with a wooden head.
In anger Pinocchio hit the Cricket, straight on its head with a hammer. The poor Cricket fell from the wall, dead!
cri-cri-cri
After a while, Pinocchio started looking for food, for he was hungry. But...
Oh! The pot is empty!
If I could find even a cookie!
Or at least a piece of dried bread!
A bone left by the dog would taste good!
But it was not enough for poor Pinocchio and he remained hungry.

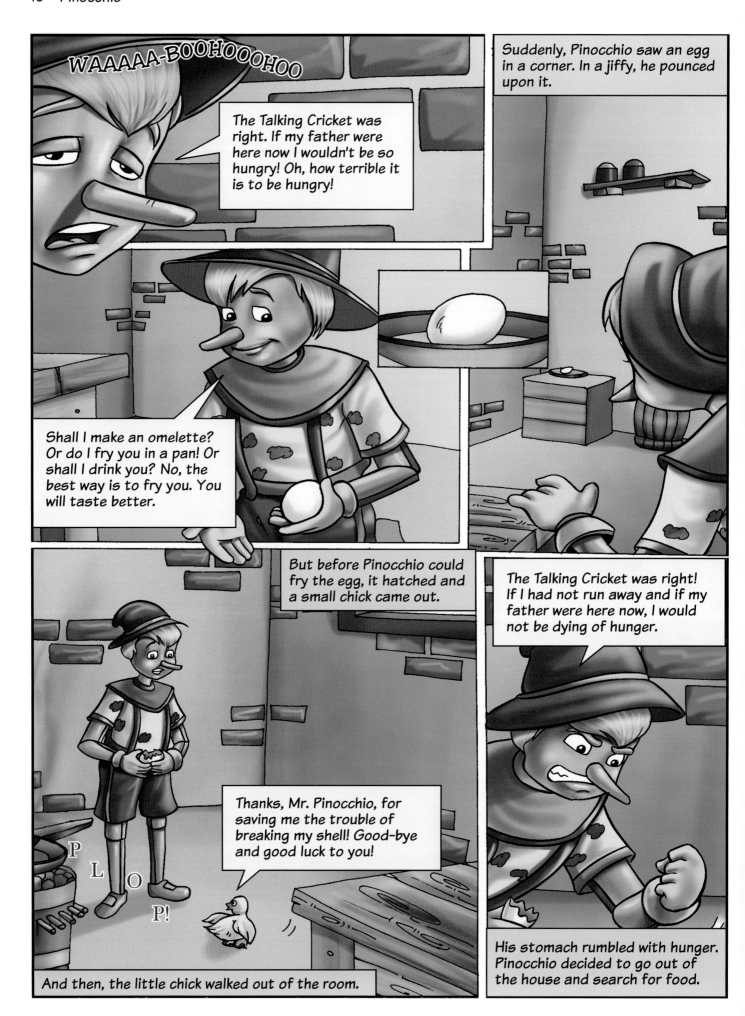

WAAAAA-BOOHOOOHOO

The Talking Cricket was right. If my father were here now I wouldn't be so hungry! Oh, how terrible it is to be hungry!

Shall I make an omelette? Or do I fry you in a pan! Or shall I drink you? No, the best way is to fry you. You will taste better.

Suddenly, Pinocchio saw an egg in a corner. In a jiffy, he pounced upon it.

But before Pinocchio could fry the egg, it hatched and a small chick came out.

The Talking Cricket was right! If I had not run away and if my father were here now, I would not be dying of hunger.

P L O P!

Thanks, Mr. Pinocchio, for saving me the trouble of breaking my shell! Good-bye and good luck to you!

And then, the little chick walked out of the room.

His stomach rumbled with hunger. Pinocchio decided to go out of the house and search for food.

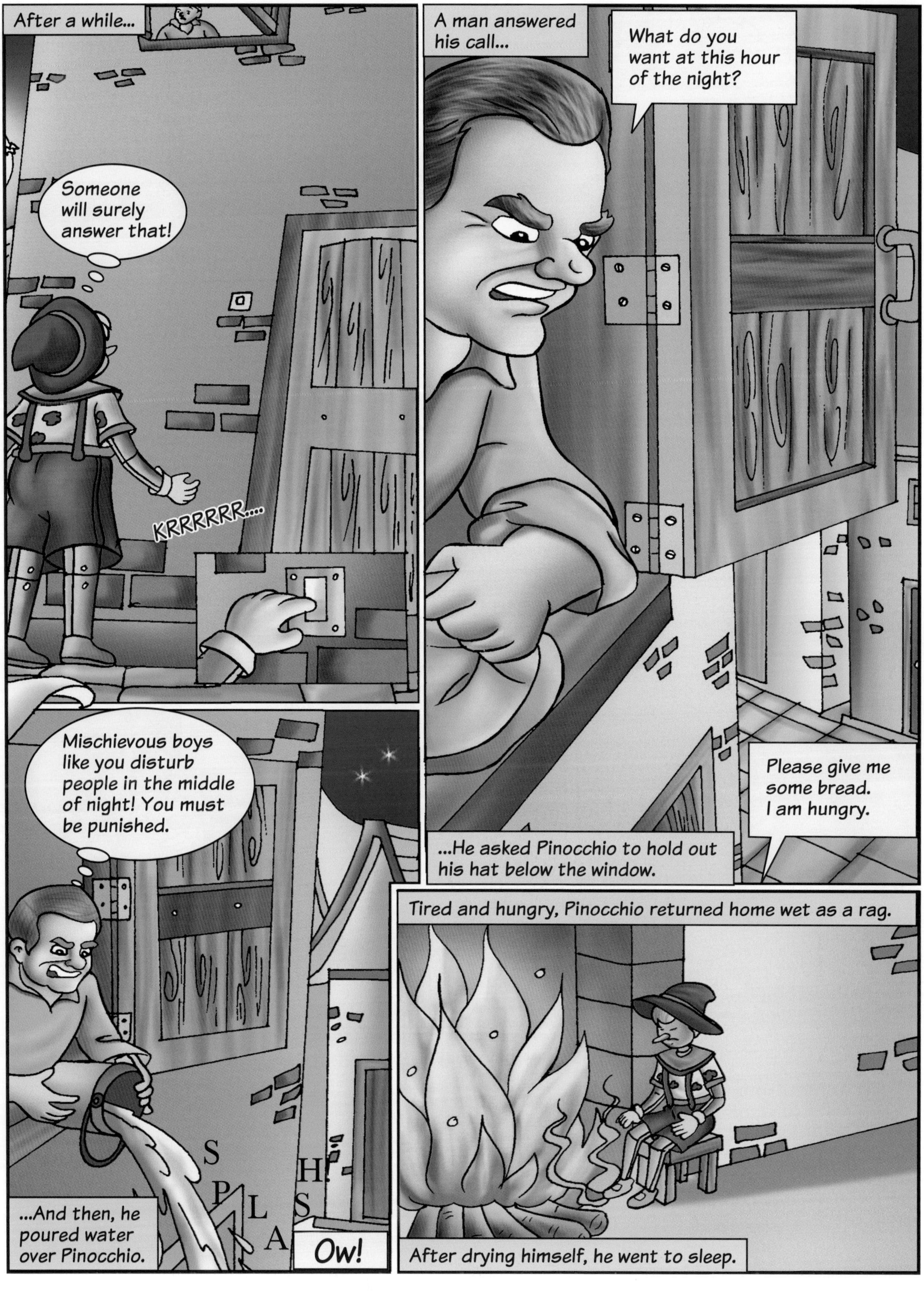
After a while...
Someone will surely answer that!
KRRRRRR....
A man answered his call...
What do you want at this hour of the night?
Please give me some bread. I am hungry.
...He asked Pinocchio to hold out his hat below the window.
Mischievous boys like you disturb people in the middle of night! You must be punished.
...And then, he poured water over Pinocchio.
SPLASH!
Ow!
Tired and hungry, Pinocchio returned home wet as a rag.
After drying himself, he went to sleep.

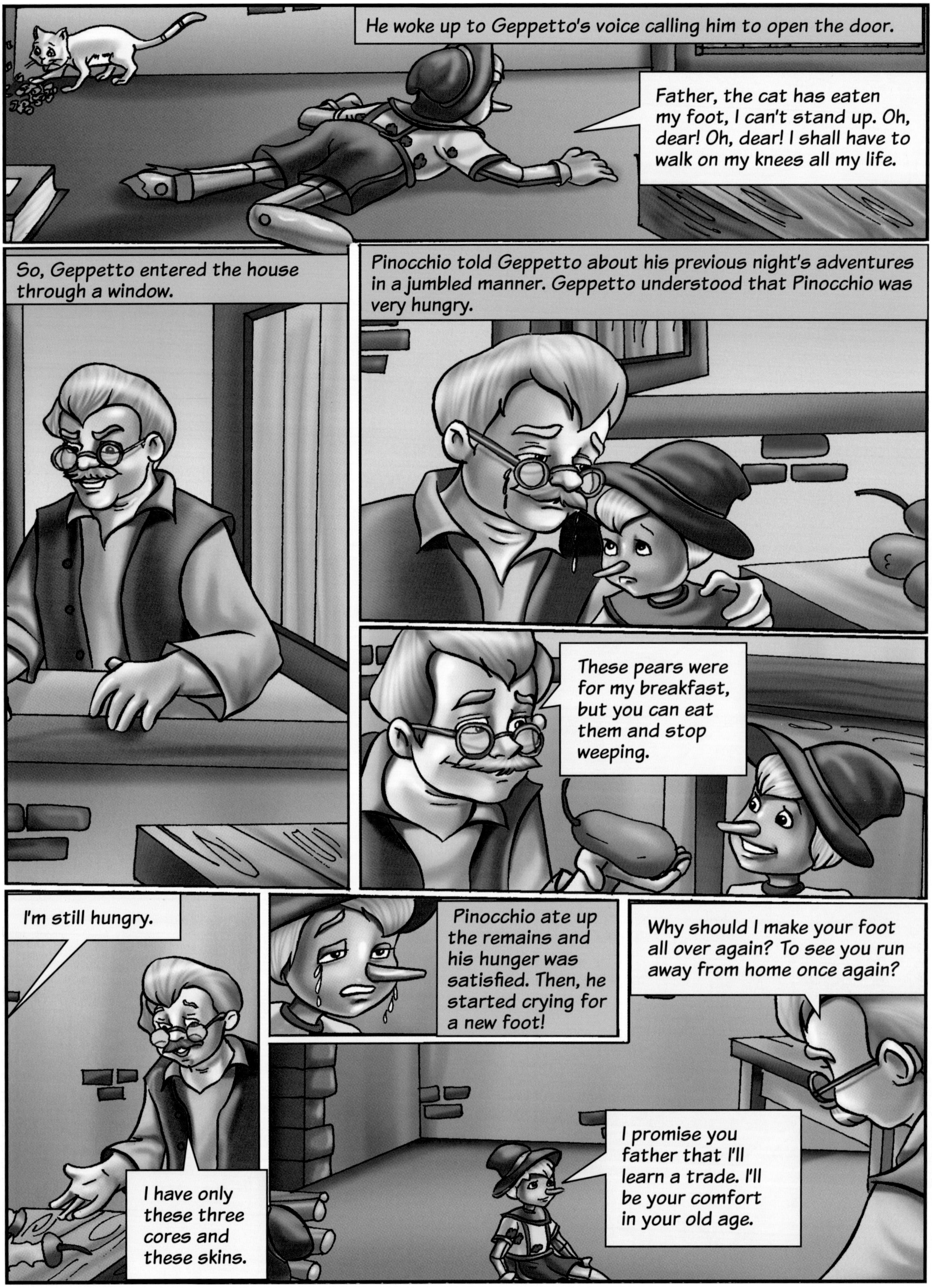
He woke up to Geppetto's voice calling him to open the door.
Father, the cat has eaten my foot, I can't stand up. Oh, dear! Oh, dear! I shall have to walk on my knees all my life.
So, Geppetto entered the house through a window.
Pinocchio told Geppetto about his previous night's adventures in a jumbled manner. Geppetto understood that Pinocchio was very hungry.
These pears were for my breakfast, but you can eat them and stop weeping.
I'm still hungry.
I have only these three cores and these skins.
Pinocchio ate up the remains and his hunger was satisfied. Then, he started crying for a new foot!
Why should I make your foot all over again? To see you run away from home once again?
I promise you father that I'll learn a trade. I'll be your comfort in your old age.

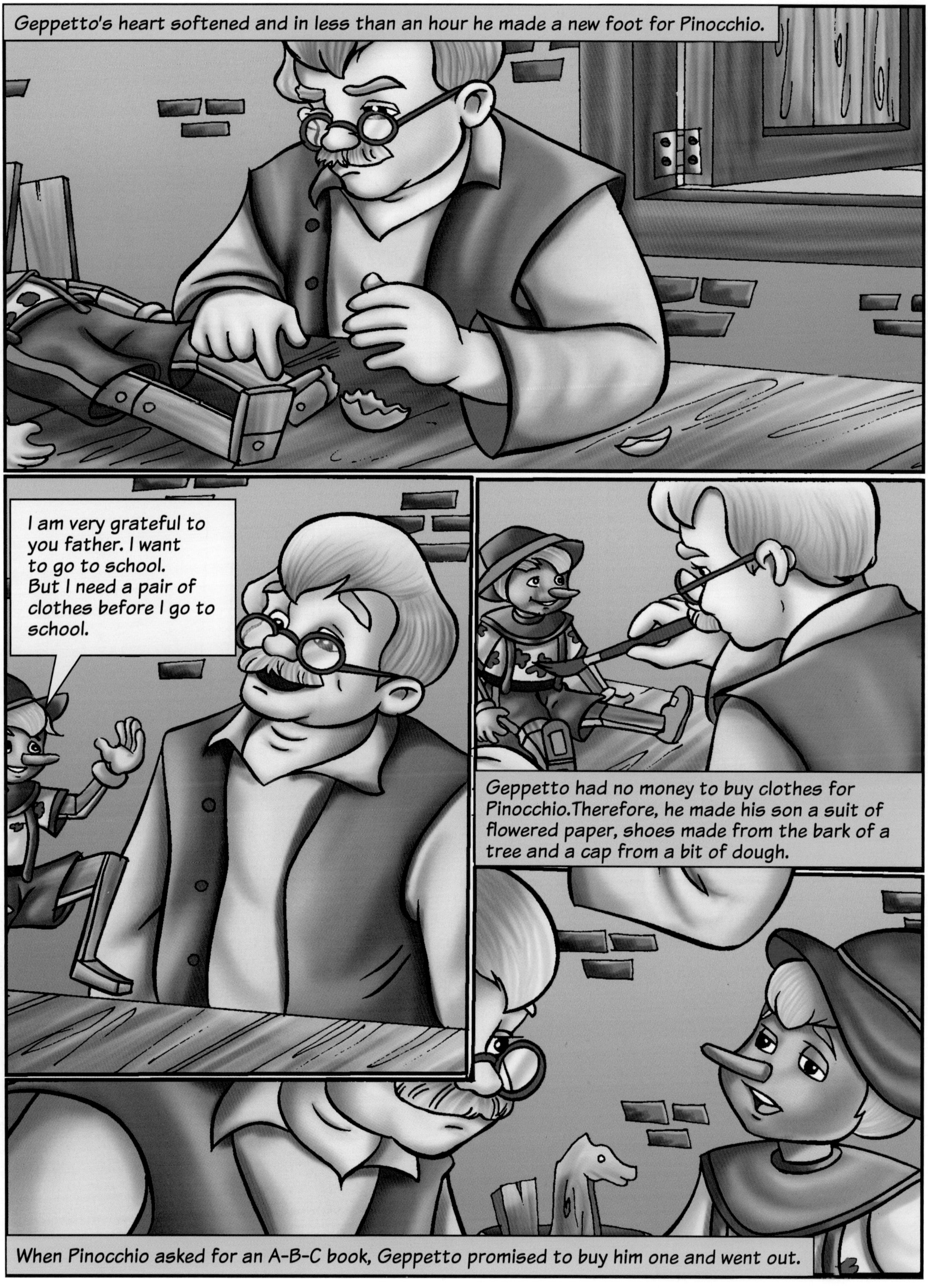
Geppetto's heart softened and in less than an hour he made a new foot for Pinocchio.
I am very grateful to you father. I want to go to school. But I need a pair of clothes before I go to school.
Geppetto had no money to buy clothes for Pinocchio.Therefore, he made his son a suit of flowered paper, shoes made from the bark of a tree and a cap from a bit of dough.
When Pinocchio asked for an A-B-C book, Geppetto promised to buy him one and went out.

Geppetto returned a few hours later, with the A-B-C book.

My A-B-C book! But where's your coat, Father?

I have sold it. It was too warm.

Pinocchio was unable to restrain his tears. He jumped on his father's neck and kissed him over and over.

Next morning, Pinocchio went towards school, building hundreds of castles in the air.

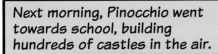

In school I'll learn to read, write and then earn a lot of money.

I'll buy Father a gold and silver coat with diamond buttons.

pi-pi-pi pi-pi-pi...zum zum zum zum

Suddenly, Pinocchio heard the sound of pipes and decided to follow them.

pi-pi-pi   pi-pi-pi...zum zum zum zum

Today I'll follow the pipes. Tomorrow I'll go to school.

GREAT MARIONET THEATER

Pinocchio ran towards the magical sounds and reached a big square full of people.

Pinocchio didn't have four pennies required to enter the show, so...

Will you give me four pennies for my coat?

I'll give you four pennies for your A-B-C book.

The book changed hands. Poor old Geppetto sat at home in his shirt shivering with cold as he had sold his coat to buy that little book for his son!

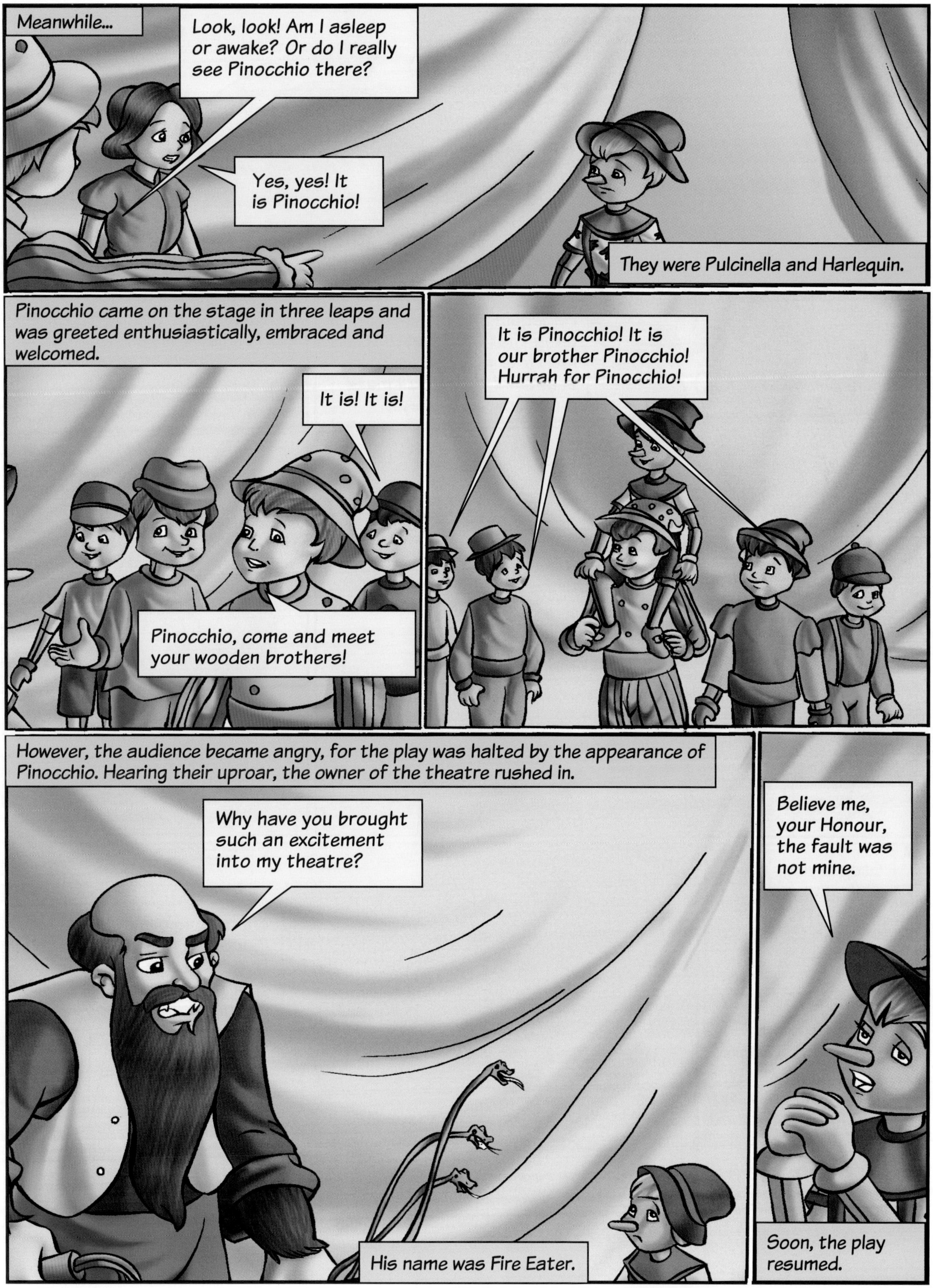
Meanwhile...
Look, look! Am I asleep or awake? Or do I really see Pinocchio there?
Yes, yes! It is Pinocchio!
They were Pulcinella and Harlequin.
Pinocchio came on the stage in three leaps and was greeted enthusiastically, embraced and welcomed.
It is! It is!
Pinocchio, come and meet your wooden brothers!
It is Pinocchio! It is our brother Pinocchio! Hurrah for Pinocchio!
However, the audience became angry, for the play was halted by the appearance of Pinocchio. Hearing their uproar, the owner of the theatre rushed in.
Why have you brought such an excitement into my theatre?
His name was Fire Eater.
Believe me, your Honour, the fault was not mine.
Soon, the play resumed.

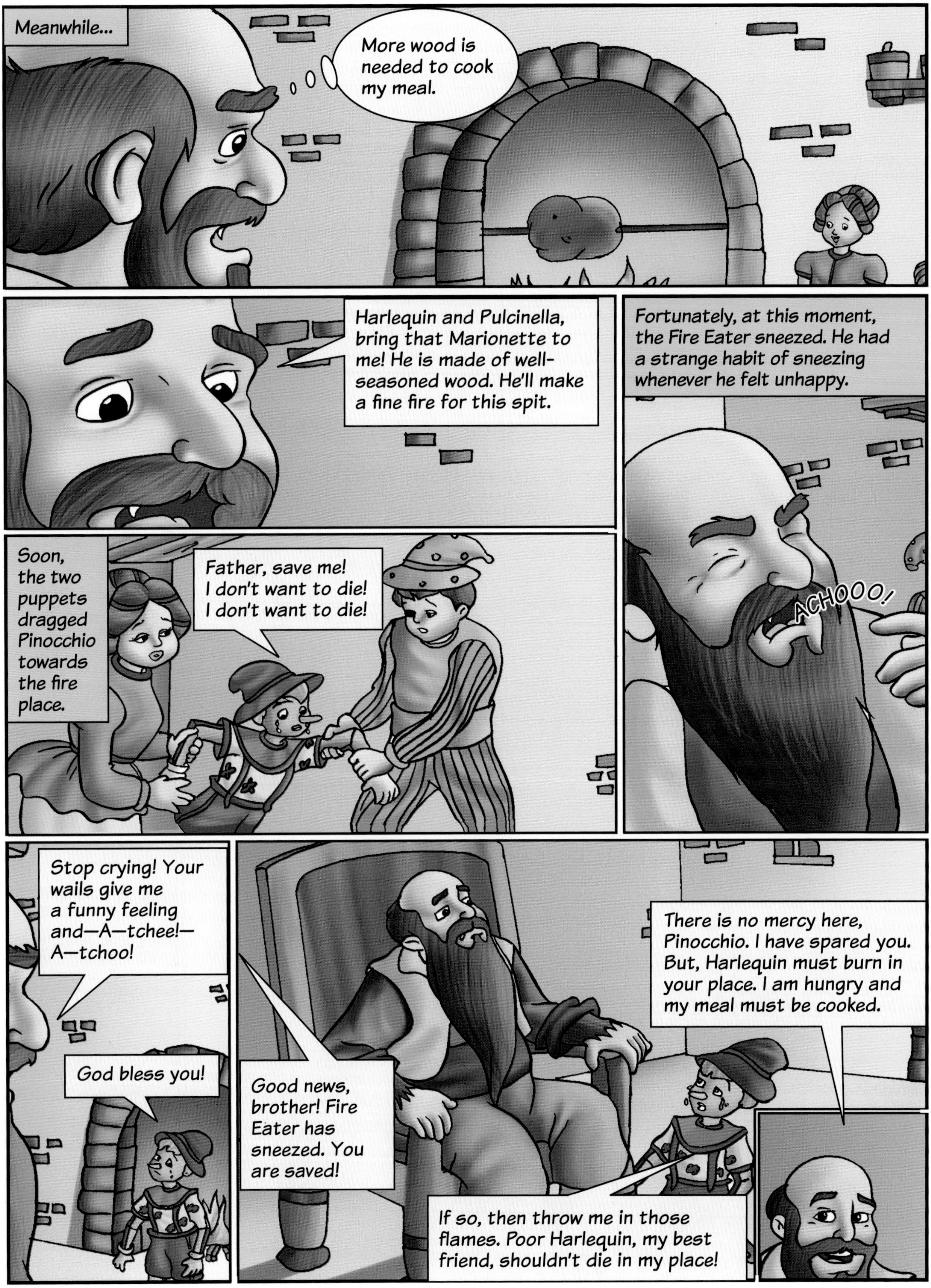
Meanwhile...
More wood is needed to cook my meal.
Harlequin and Pulcinella, bring that Marionette to me! He is made of well-seasoned wood. He'll make a fine fire for this spit.
Fortunately, at this moment, the Fire Eater sneezed. He had a strange habit of sneezing whenever he felt unhappy.
Soon, the two puppets dragged Pinocchio towards the fire place.
Father, save me! I don't want to die! I don't want to die!
ACHOOO!
Stop crying! Your wails give me a funny feeling and—A—tchee!—A—tchoo!
God bless you!
Good news, brother! Fire Eater has sneezed. You are saved!
There is no mercy here, Pinocchio. I have spared you. But, Harlequin must burn in your place. I am hungry and my meal must be cooked.
If so, then throw me in those flames. Poor Harlequin, my best friend, shouldn't die in my place!

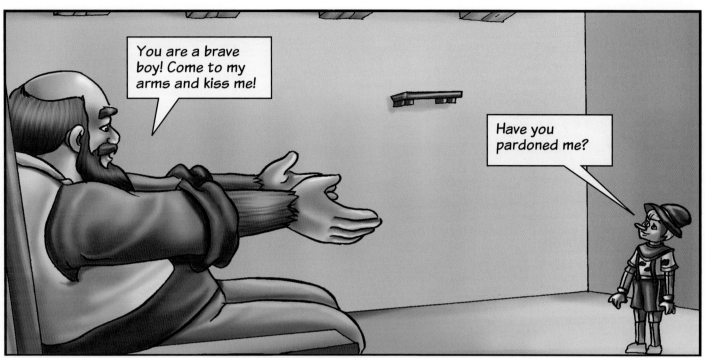

You are a brave boy! Come to my arms and kiss me!

Have you pardoned me?

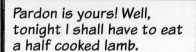

Pardon is yours! Well, tonight I shall have to eat a half cooked lamb.

Then, the Fire Eater inquired about Pinocchio's father.

My father, Geppetto never has a penny in his pockets. In order to buy me an A-B-C book for school, he sold his only coat.

Poor fellow! I feel sorry for him. Take these five gold pieces. Go, give them to him with my kindest regards.

Pinocchio joyfully set out towards home.

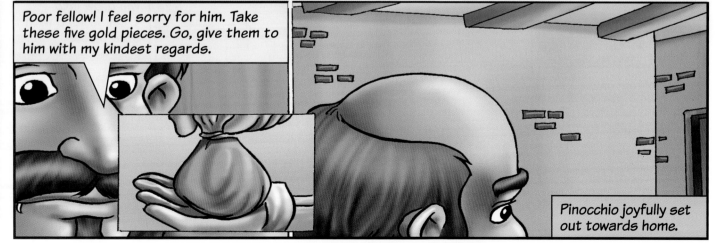

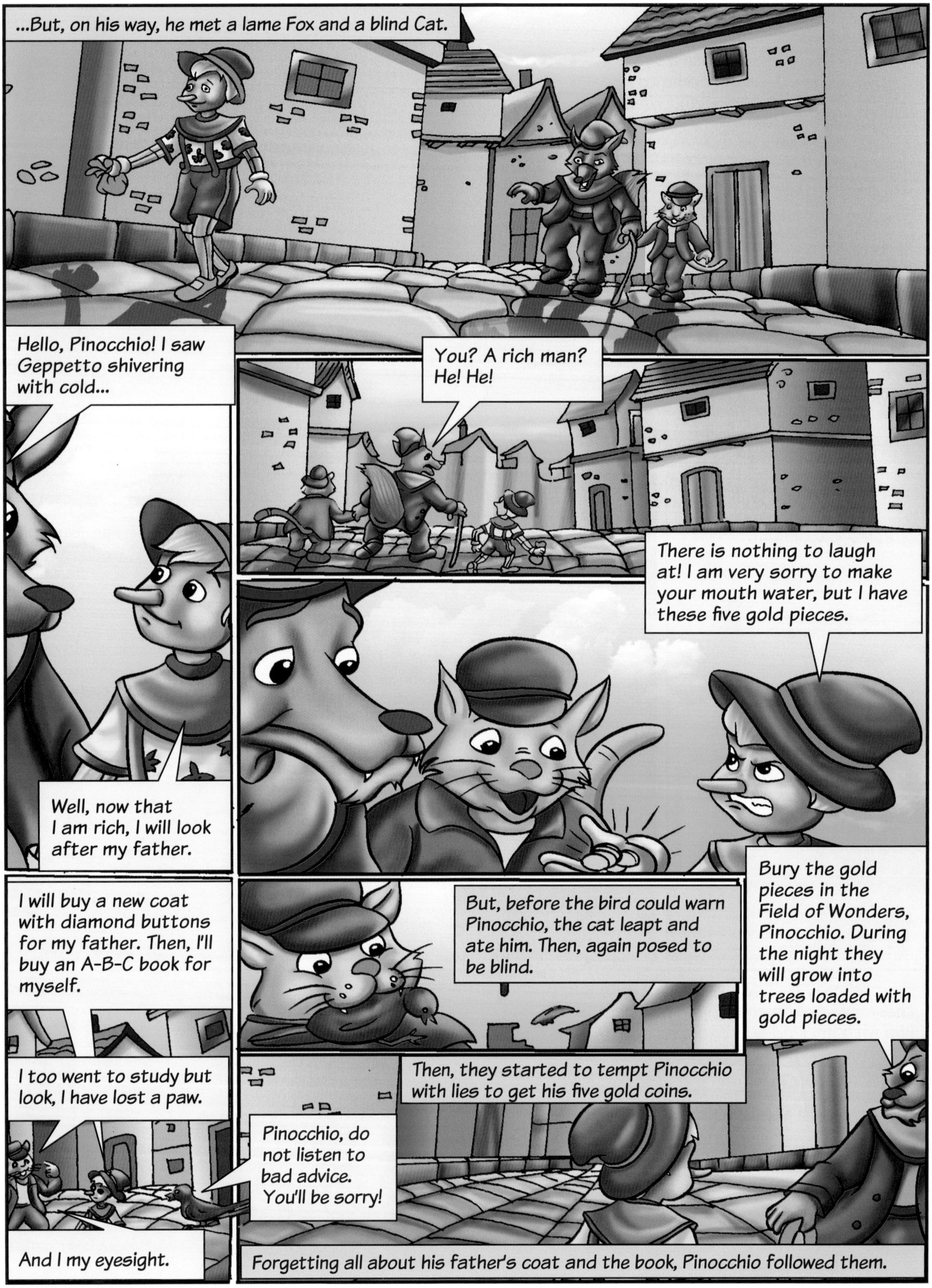
...But, on his way, he met a lame Fox and a blind Cat.
Hello, Pinocchio! I saw Geppetto shivering with cold...
Well, now that I am rich, I will look after my father.
You? A rich man? He! He!
There is nothing to laugh at! I am very sorry to make your mouth water, but I have these five gold pieces.
I will buy a new coat with diamond buttons for my father. Then, I'll buy an A-B-C book for myself.
I too went to study but look, I have lost a paw.
And I my eyesight.
Pinocchio, do not listen to bad advice. You'll be sorry!
But, before the bird could warn Pinocchio, the cat leapt and ate him. Then, again posed to be blind.
Bury the gold pieces in the Field of Wonders, Pinocchio. During the night they will grow into trees loaded with gold pieces.
Then, they started to tempt Pinocchio with lies to get his five gold coins.
Forgetting all about his father's coat and the book, Pinocchio followed them.

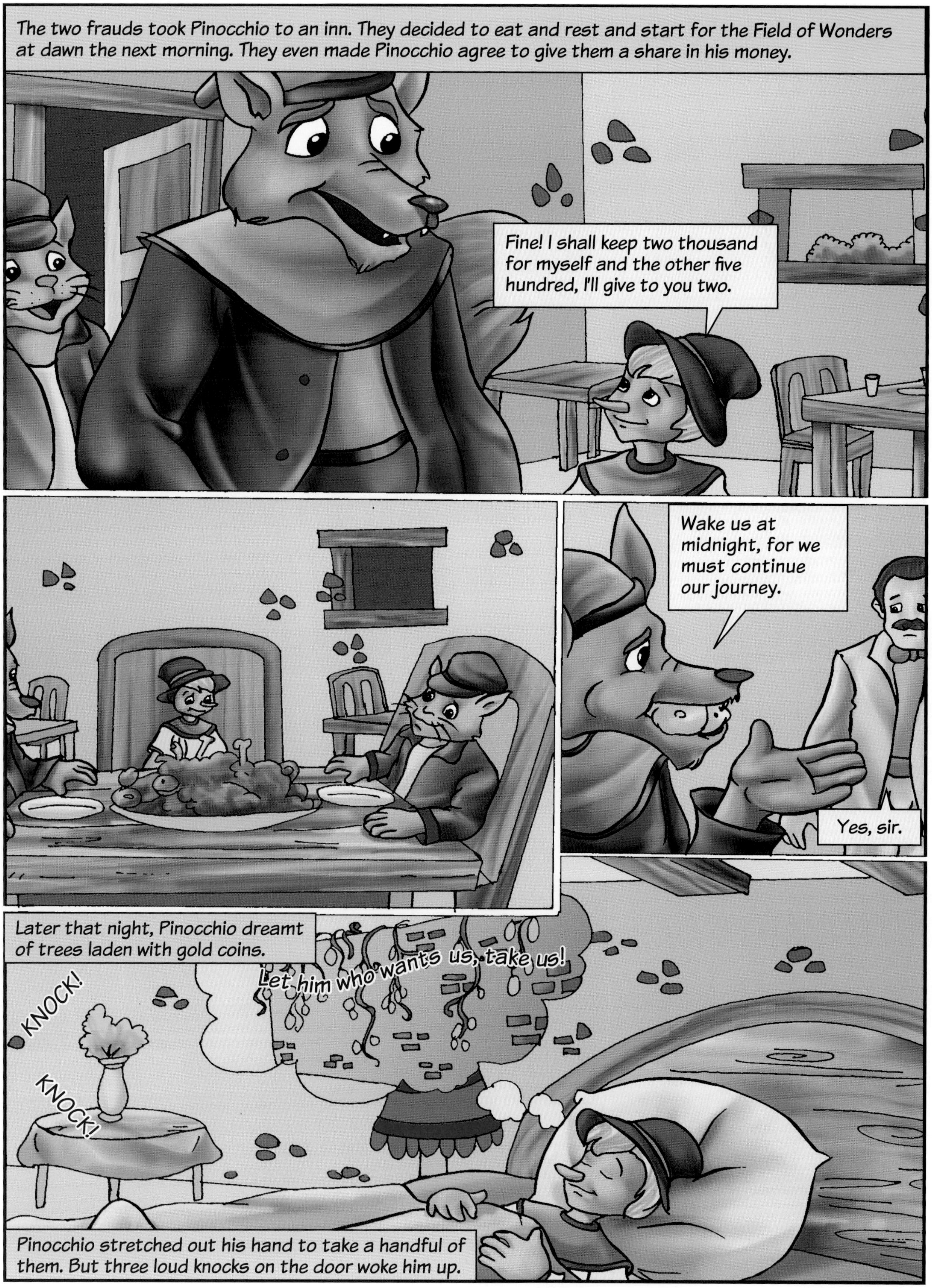
The two frauds took Pinocchio to an inn. They decided to eat and rest and start for the Field of Wonders at dawn the next morning. They even made Pinocchio agree to give them a share in his money.
Fine! I shall keep two thousand for myself and the other five hundred, I'll give to you two.
Wake us at midnight, for we must continue our journey.
Yes, sir.
Later that night, Pinocchio dreamt of trees laden with gold coins.
Let him who wants us, take us!
KNOCK!
KNOCK!
Pinocchio stretched out his hand to take a handful of them. But three loud knocks on the door woke him up.

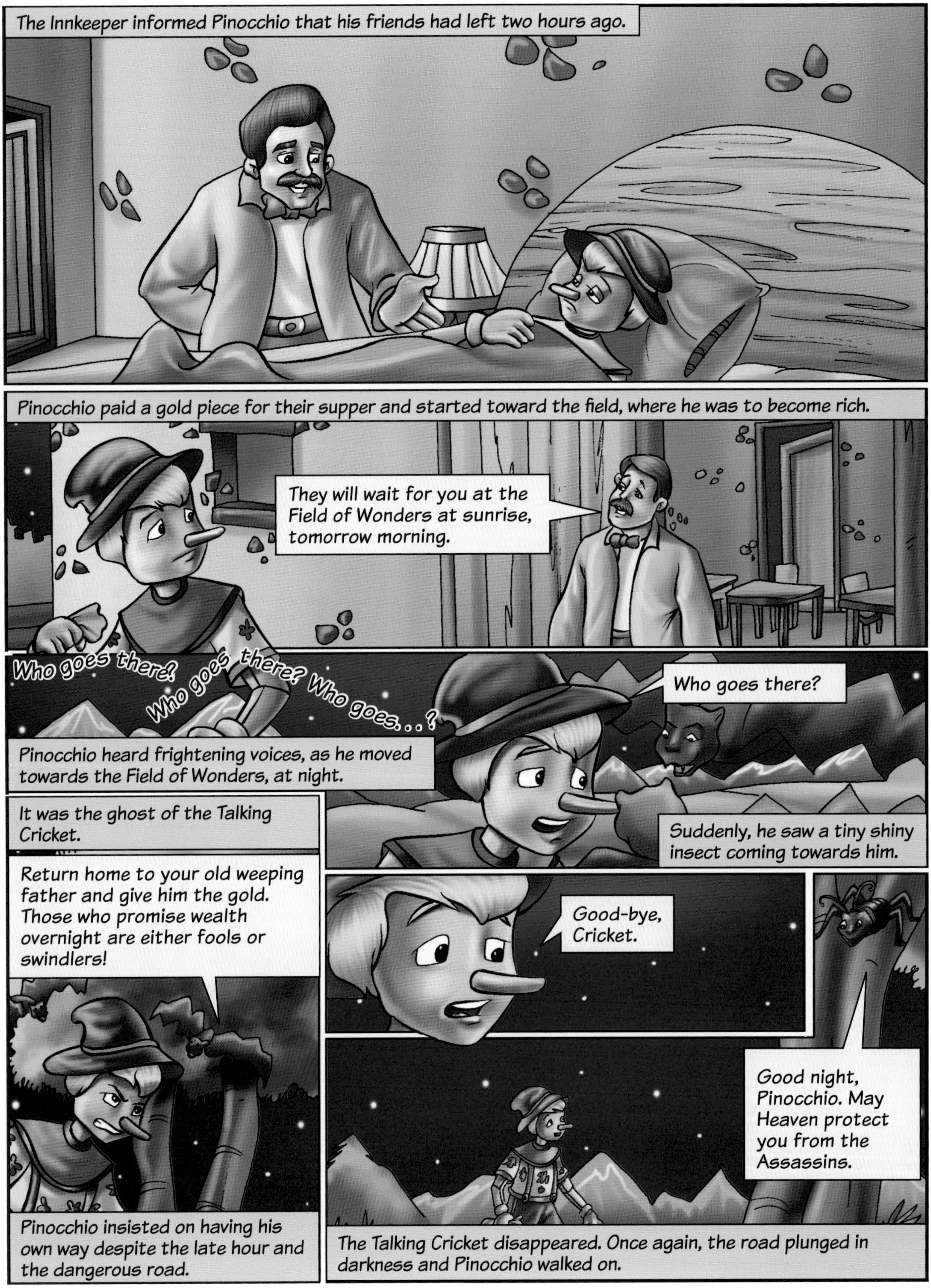

The Innkeeper informed Pinocchio that his friends had left two hours ago.
Pinocchio paid a gold piece for their supper and started toward the field, where he was to become rich.
They will wait for you at the Field of Wonders at sunrise, tomorrow morning.
Who goes there? Who goes there? Who goes...?
Who goes there?
Pinocchio heard frightening voices, as he moved towards the Field of Wonders, at night.
Suddenly, he saw a tiny shiny insect coming towards him.
It was the ghost of the Talking Cricket.
Return home to your old weeping father and give him the gold. Those who promise wealth overnight are either fools or swindlers!
Pinocchio insisted on having his own way despite the late hour and the dangerous road.
Good-bye, Cricket.
Good night, Pinocchio. May Heaven protect you from the Assassins.
The Talking Cricket disappeared. Once again, the road plunged in darkness and Pinocchio walked on.

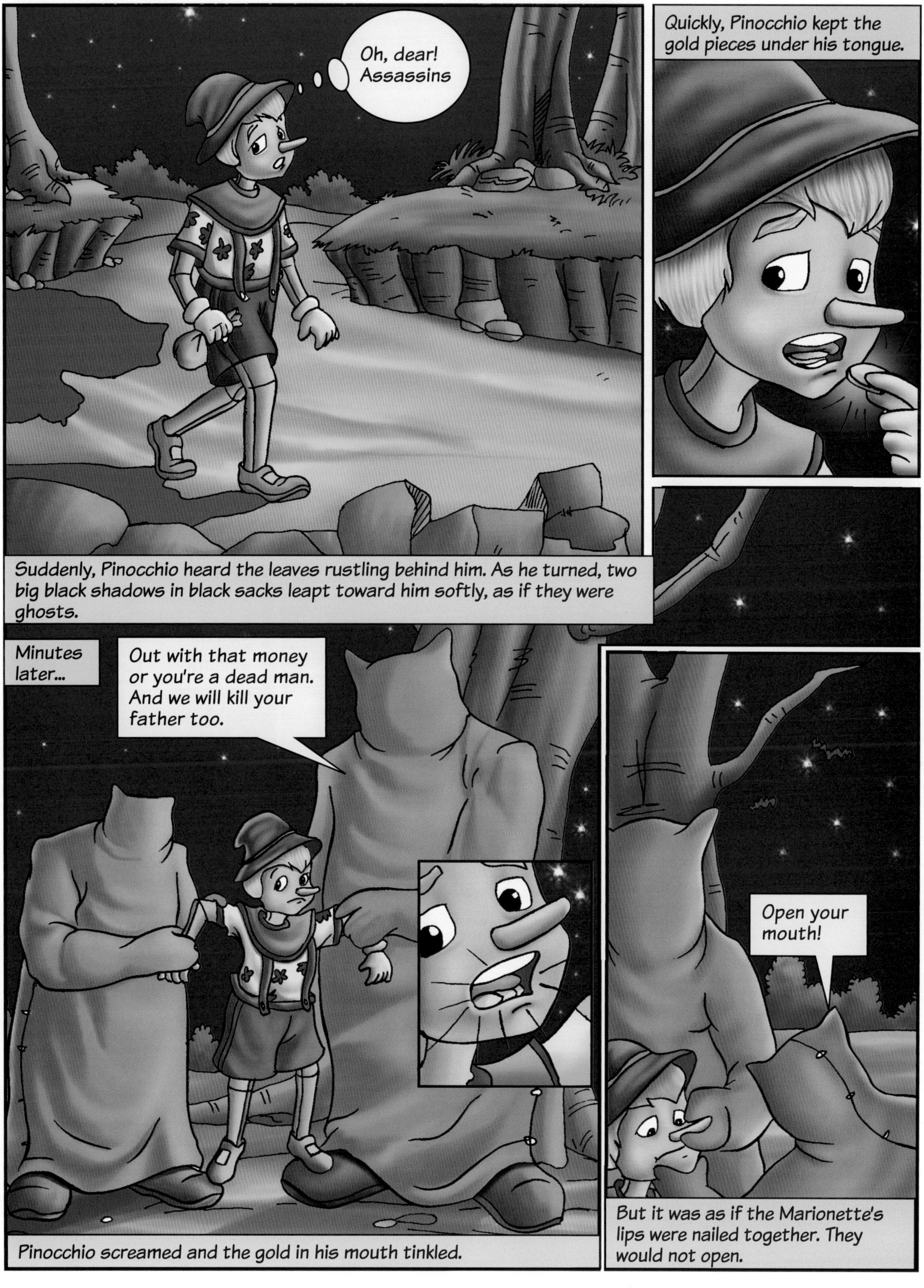
Oh, dear! Assassins
Suddenly, Pinocchio heard the leaves rustling behind him. As he turned, two big black shadows in black sacks leapt toward him softly, as if they were ghosts.
Quickly, Pinocchio kept the gold pieces under his tongue.
Minutes later...
Out with that money or you're a dead man. And we will kill your father too.
Pinocchio screamed and the gold in his mouth tinkled.
Open your mouth!
But it was as if the Marionette's lips were nailed together. They would not open.

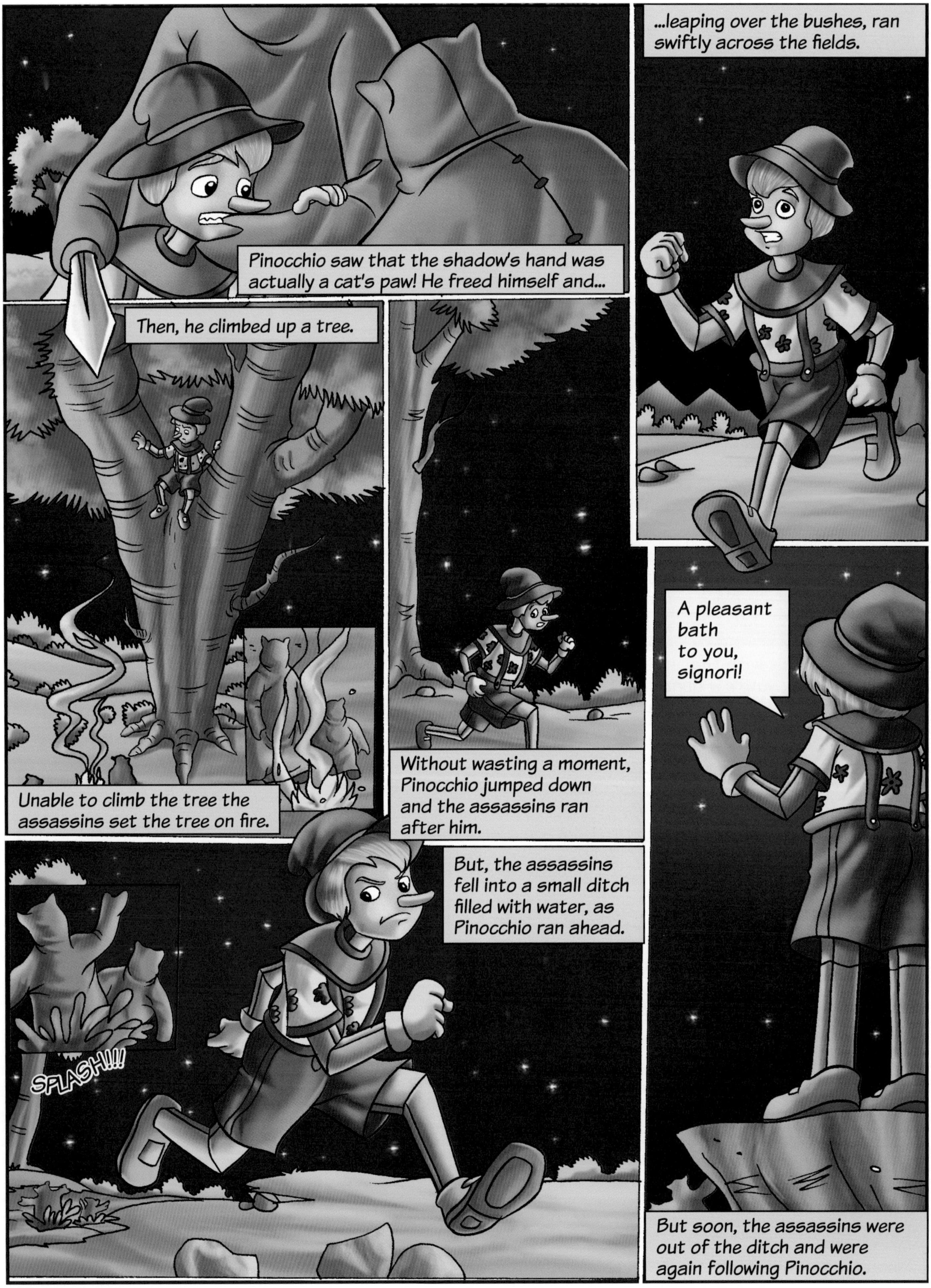
Pinocchio saw that the shadow's hand was actually a cat's paw! He freed himself and...
...leaping over the bushes, ran swiftly across the fields.
Then, he climbed up a tree.
Unable to climb the tree the assassins set the tree on fire.
Without wasting a moment, Pinocchio jumped down and the assassins ran after him.
But, the assassins fell into a small ditch filled with water, as Pinocchio ran ahead.
SPLASH!!!
A pleasant bath to you, signori!
But soon, the assassins were out of the ditch and were again following Pinocchio.

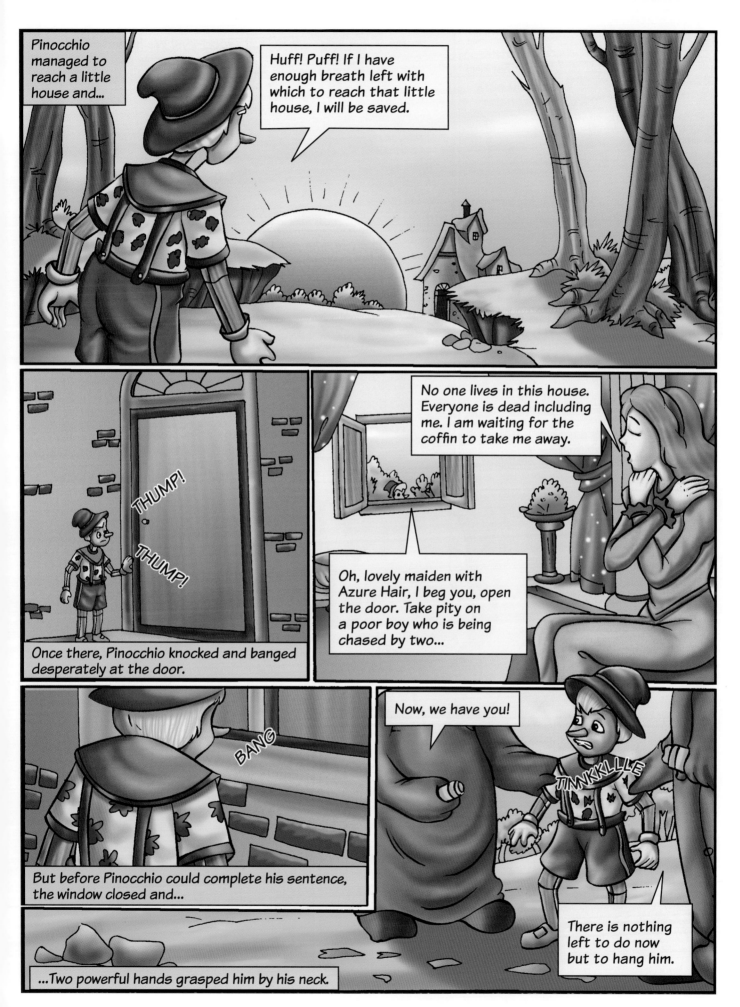

Pinocchio managed to reach a little house and...

Huff! Puff! If I have enough breath left with which to reach that little house, I will be saved.

Once there, Pinocchio knocked and banged desperately at the door.

THUMP!

THUMP!

No one lives in this house. Everyone is dead including me. I am waiting for the coffin to take me away.

Oh, lovely maiden with Azure Hair, I beg you, open the door. Take pity on a poor boy who is being chased by two...

But before Pinocchio could complete his sentence, the window closed and...

BANG

...Two powerful hands grasped him by his neck.

Now, we have you!

TINNKKLLLE

There is nothing left to do now but to hang him.

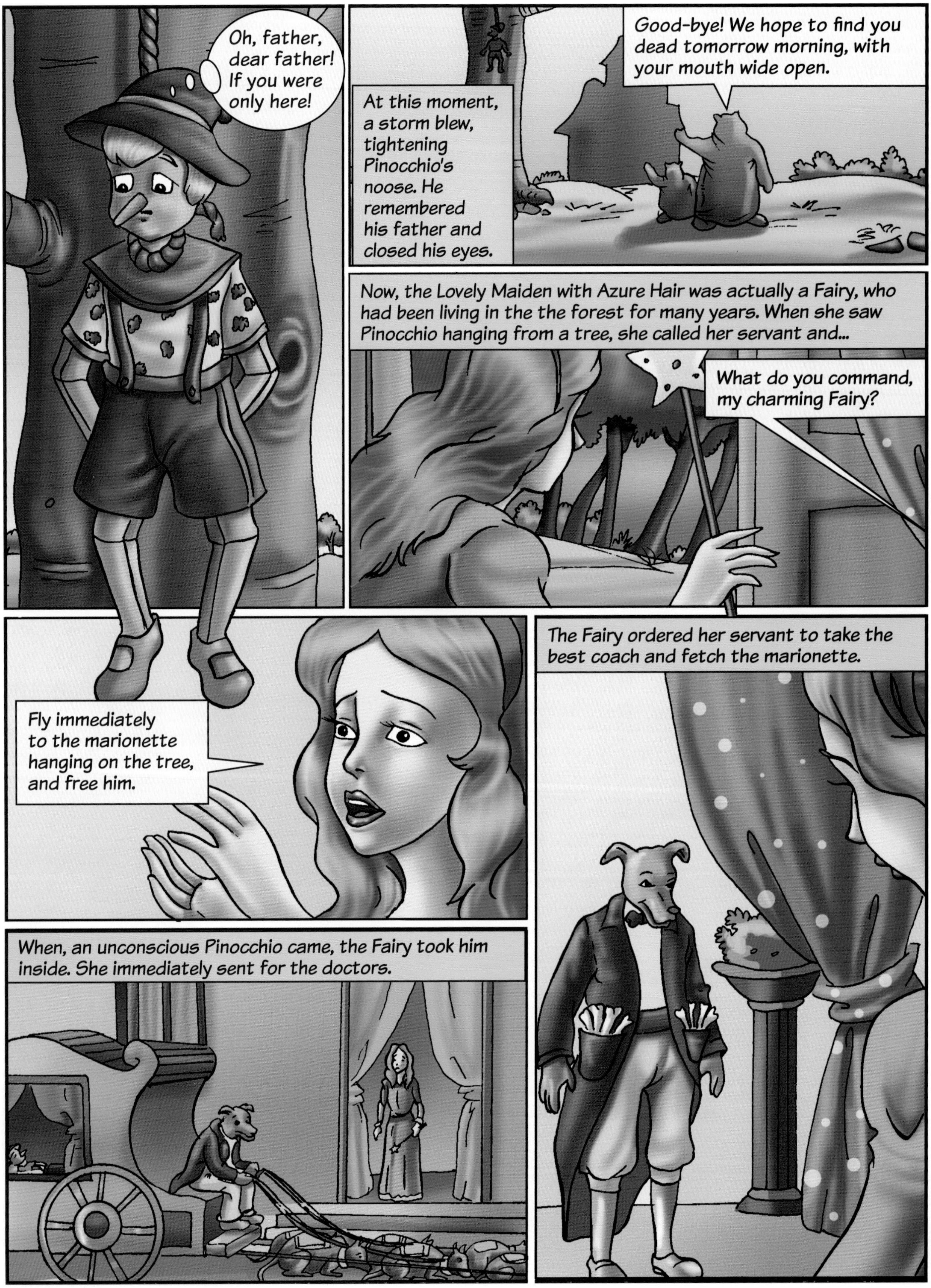
Oh, father, dear father! If you were only here!
At this moment, a storm blew, tightening Pinocchio's noose. He remembered his father and closed his eyes.
Good-bye! We hope to find you dead tomorrow morning, with your mouth wide open.
Now, the Lovely Maiden with Azure Hair was actually a Fairy, who had been living in the the forest for many years. When she saw Pinocchio hanging from a tree, she called her servant and...
What do you command, my charming Fairy?
Fly immediately to the marionette hanging on the tree, and free him.
The Fairy ordered her servant to take the best coach and fetch the marionette.
When, an unconscious Pinocchio came, the Fairy took him inside. She immediately sent for the doctors.

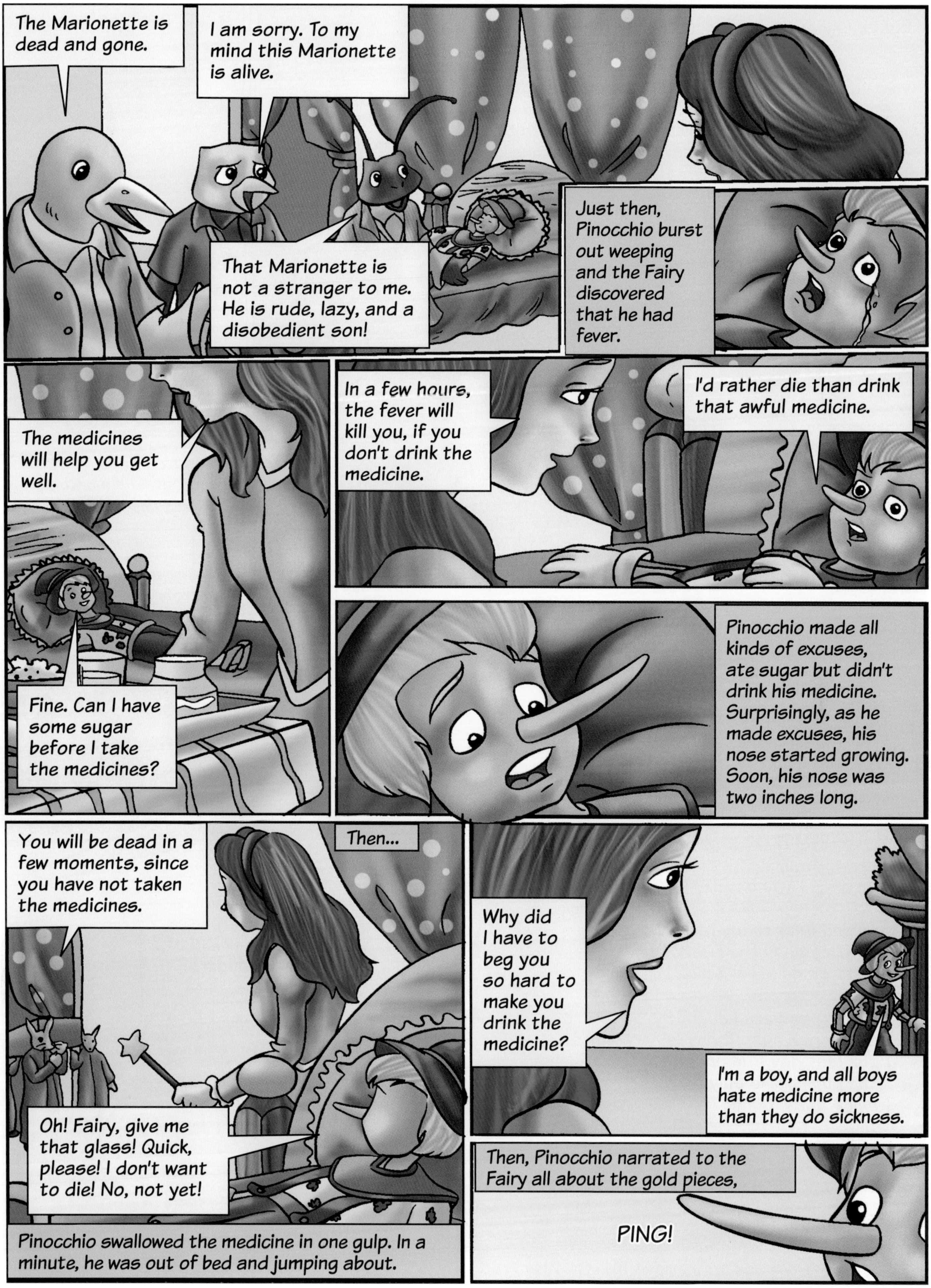
The Marionette is dead and gone.
I am sorry. To my mind this Marionette is alive.
That Marionette is not a stranger to me. He is rude, lazy, and a disobedient son!
Just then, Pinocchio burst out weeping and the Fairy discovered that he had fever.
The medicines will help you get well.
Fine. Can I have some sugar before I take the medicines?
In a few hours, the fever will kill you, if you don't drink the medicine.
I'd rather die than drink that awful medicine.
Pinocchio made all kinds of excuses, ate sugar but didn't drink his medicine. Surprisingly, as he made excuses, his nose started growing. Soon, his nose was two inches long.
You will be dead in a few moments, since you have not taken the medicines.
Then...
Oh! Fairy, give me that glass! Quick, please! I don't want to die! No, not yet!
Pinocchio swallowed the medicine in one gulp. In a minute, he was out of bed and jumping about.
Why did I have to beg you so hard to make you drink the medicine?
I'm a boy, and all boys hate medicine more than they do sickness.
Then, Pinocchio narrated to the Fairy all about the gold pieces,
PING!

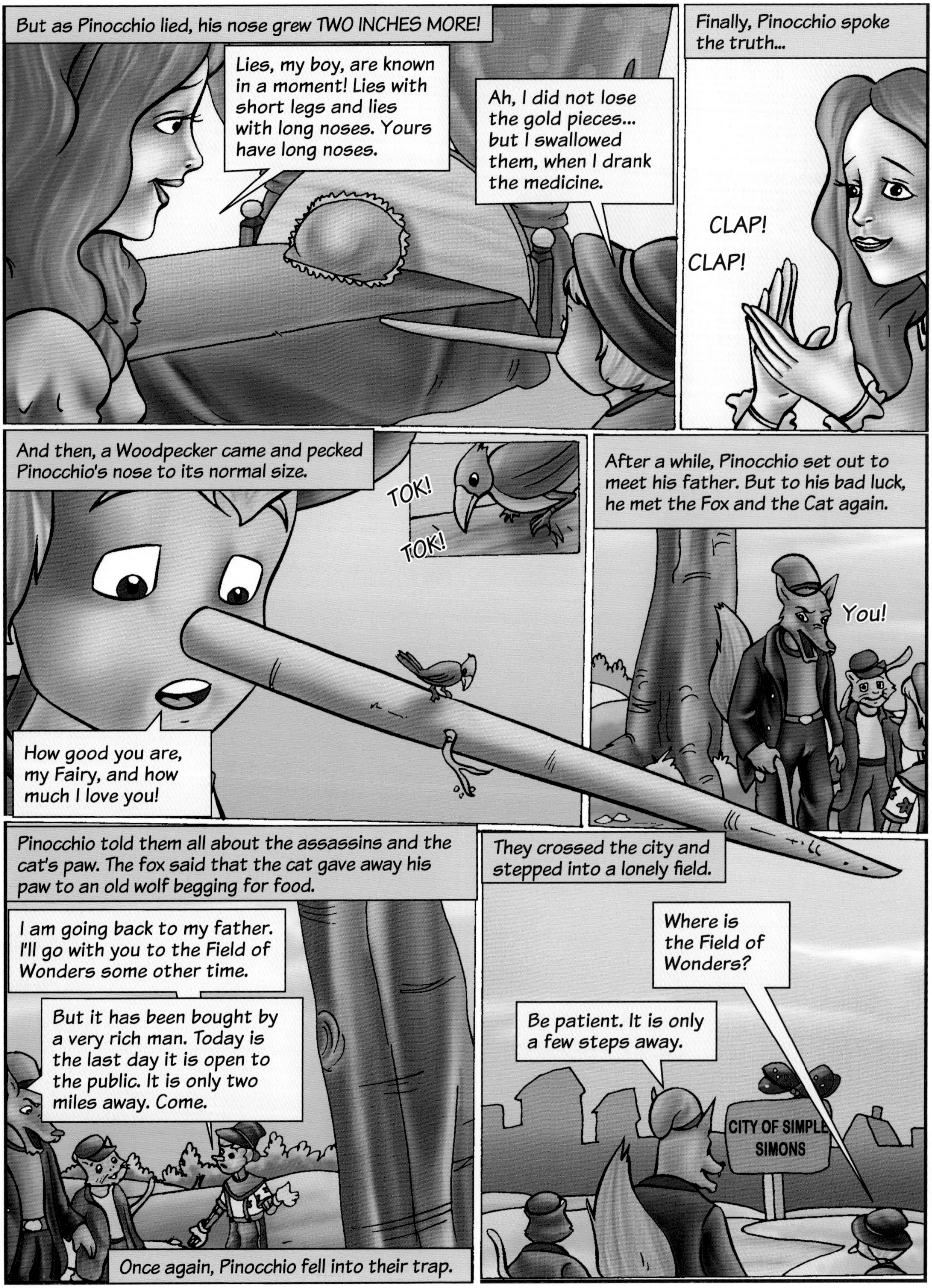
But as Pinocchio lied, his nose grew TWO INCHES MORE!
Lies, my boy, are known in a moment! Lies with short legs and lies with long noses. Yours have long noses.
Ah, I did not lose the gold pieces... but I swallowed them, when I drank the medicine.
Finally, Pinocchio spoke the truth...
CLAP!
CLAP!
And then, a Woodpecker came and pecked Pinocchio's nose to its normal size.
TOK!
TOK!
How good you are, my Fairy, and how much I love you!
After a while, Pinocchio set out to meet his father. But to his bad luck, he met the Fox and the Cat again.
You!
Pinocchio told them all about the assassins and the cat's paw. The fox said that the cat gave away his paw to an old wolf begging for food.
I am going back to my father. I'll go with you to the Field of Wonders some other time.
But it has been bought by a very rich man. Today is the last day it is open to the public. It is only two miles away. Come.
Once again, Pinocchio fell into their trap.
They crossed the city and stepped into a lonely field.
Where is the Field of Wonders?
Be patient. It is only a few steps away.
CITY OF SIMPLE SIMONS

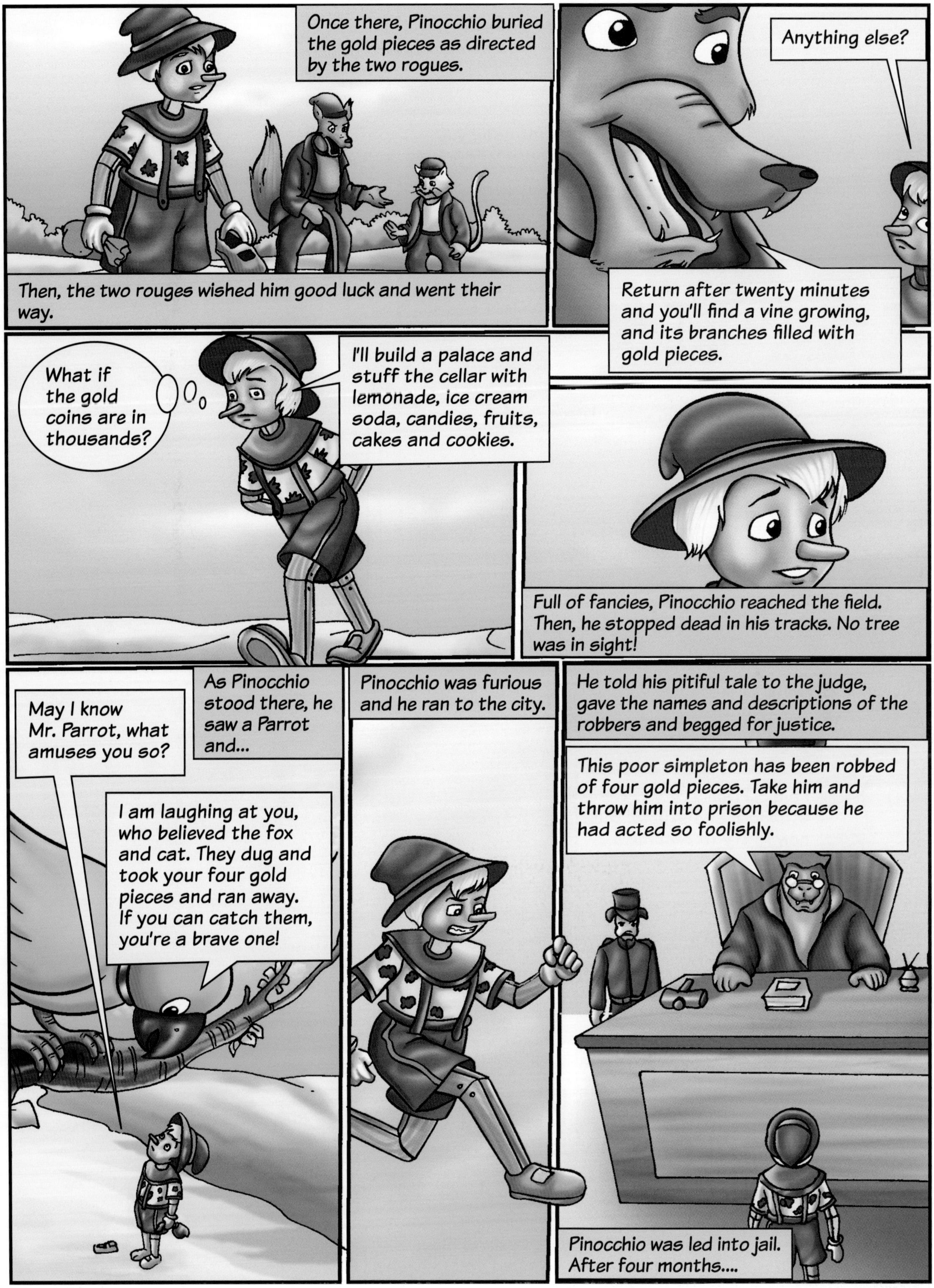
Once there, Pinocchio buried the gold pieces as directed by the two rogues.
Then, the two rouges wished him good luck and went their way.
Anything else?
Return after twenty minutes and you'll find a vine growing, and its branches filled with gold pieces.
What if the gold coins are in thousands?
I'll build a palace and stuff the cellar with lemonade, ice cream soda, candies, fruits, cakes and cookies.
Full of fancies, Pinocchio reached the field. Then, he stopped dead in his tracks. No tree was in sight!
As Pinocchio stood there, he saw a Parrot and...
May I know Mr. Parrot, what amuses you so?
I am laughing at you, who believed the fox and cat. They dug and took your four gold pieces and ran away. If you can catch them, you're a brave one!
Pinocchio was furious and he ran to the city.
He told his pitiful tale to the judge, gave the names and descriptions of the robbers and begged for justice.
This poor simpleton has been robbed of four gold pieces. Take him and throw him into prison because he had acted so foolishly.
Pinocchio was led into jail. After four months....

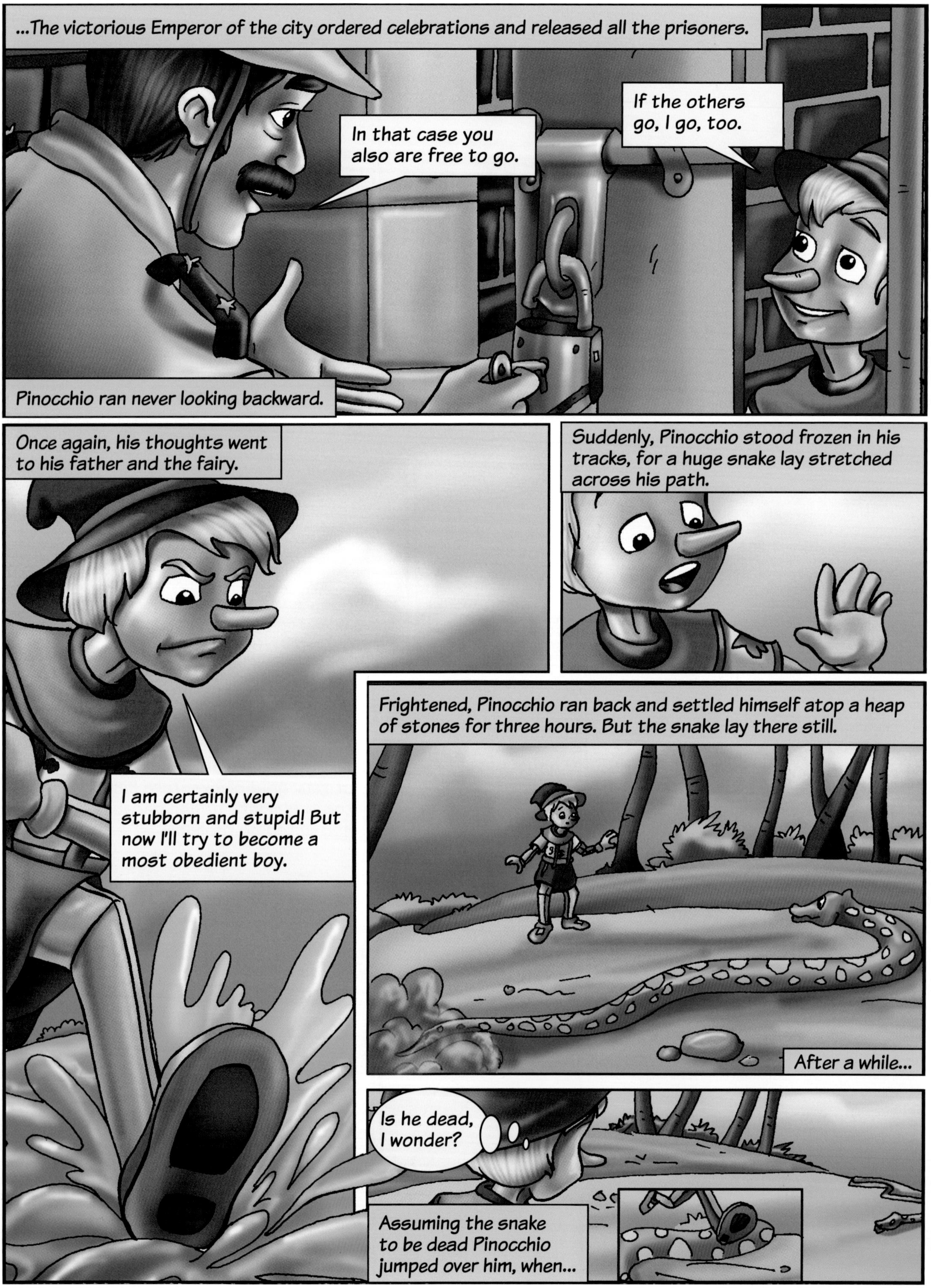
...The victorious Emperor of the city ordered celebrations and released all the prisoners.
In that case you also are free to go.
If the others go, I go, too.
Pinocchio ran never looking backward.
Once again, his thoughts went to his father and the fairy.
I am certainly very stubborn and stupid! But now I'll try to become a most obedient boy.
Suddenly, Pinocchio stood frozen in his tracks, for a huge snake lay stretched across his path.
Frightened, Pinocchio ran back and settled himself atop a heap of stones for three hours. But the snake lay there still.
After a while...
Is he dead, I wonder?
Assuming the snake to be dead Pinocchio jumped over him, when...

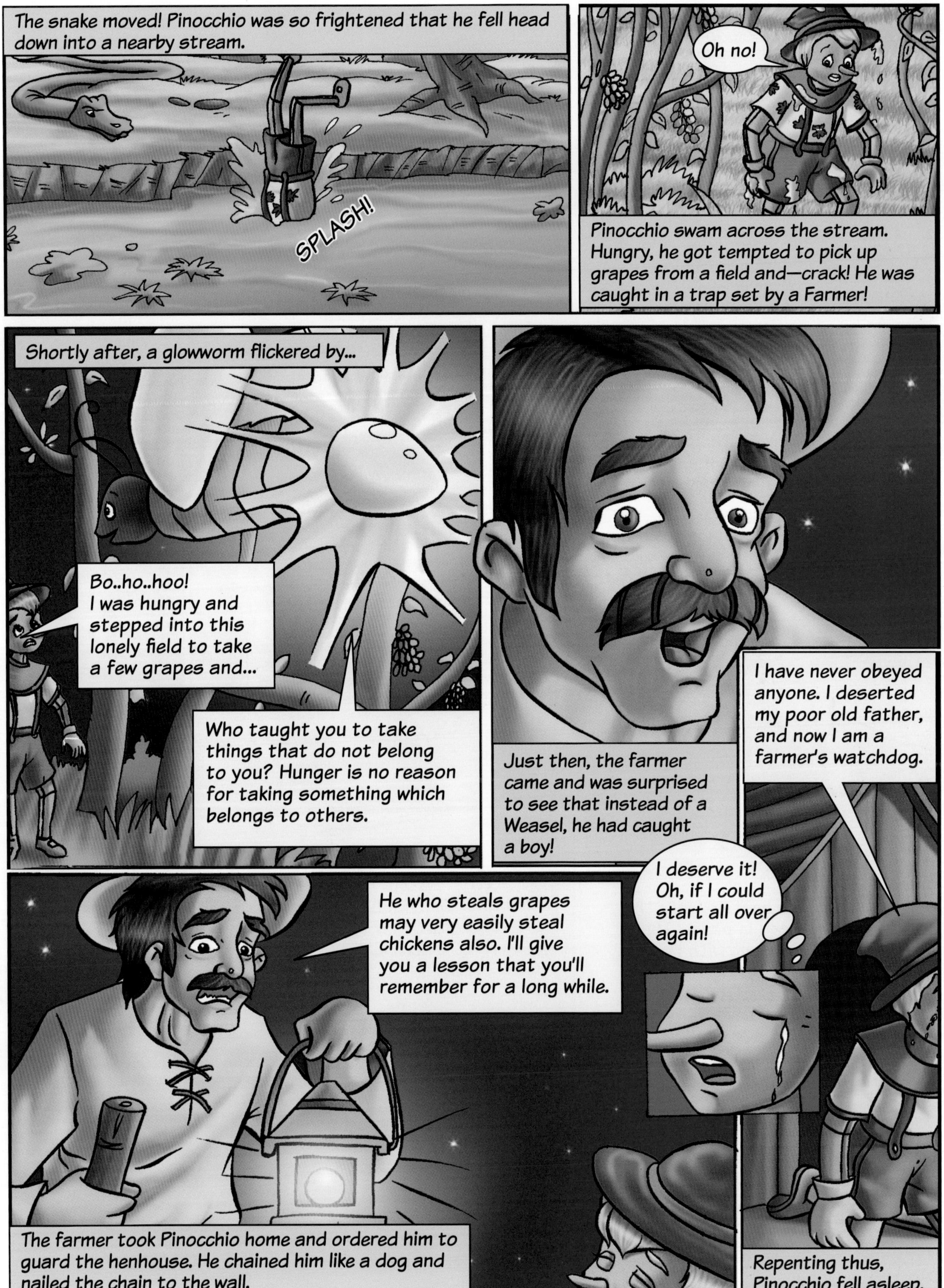
The snake moved! Pinocchio was so frightened that he fell head down into a nearby stream.
SPLASH!
Oh no!
Pinocchio swam across the stream. Hungry, he got tempted to pick up grapes from a field and—crack! He was caught in a trap set by a Farmer!
Shortly after, a glowworm flickered by...
Bo..ho..hoo! I was hungry and stepped into this lonely field to take a few grapes and...
Who taught you to take things that do not belong to you? Hunger is no reason for taking something which belongs to others.
Just then, the farmer came and was surprised to see that instead of a Weasel, he had caught a boy!
I have never obeyed anyone. I deserted my poor old father, and now I am a farmer's watchdog.
He who steals grapes may very easily steal chickens also. I'll give you a lesson that you'll remember for a long while.
The farmer took Pinocchio home and ordered him to guard the henhouse. He chained him like a dog and nailed the chain to the wall.
I deserve it! Oh, if I could start all over again!
Repenting thus, Pinocchio fell asleep.

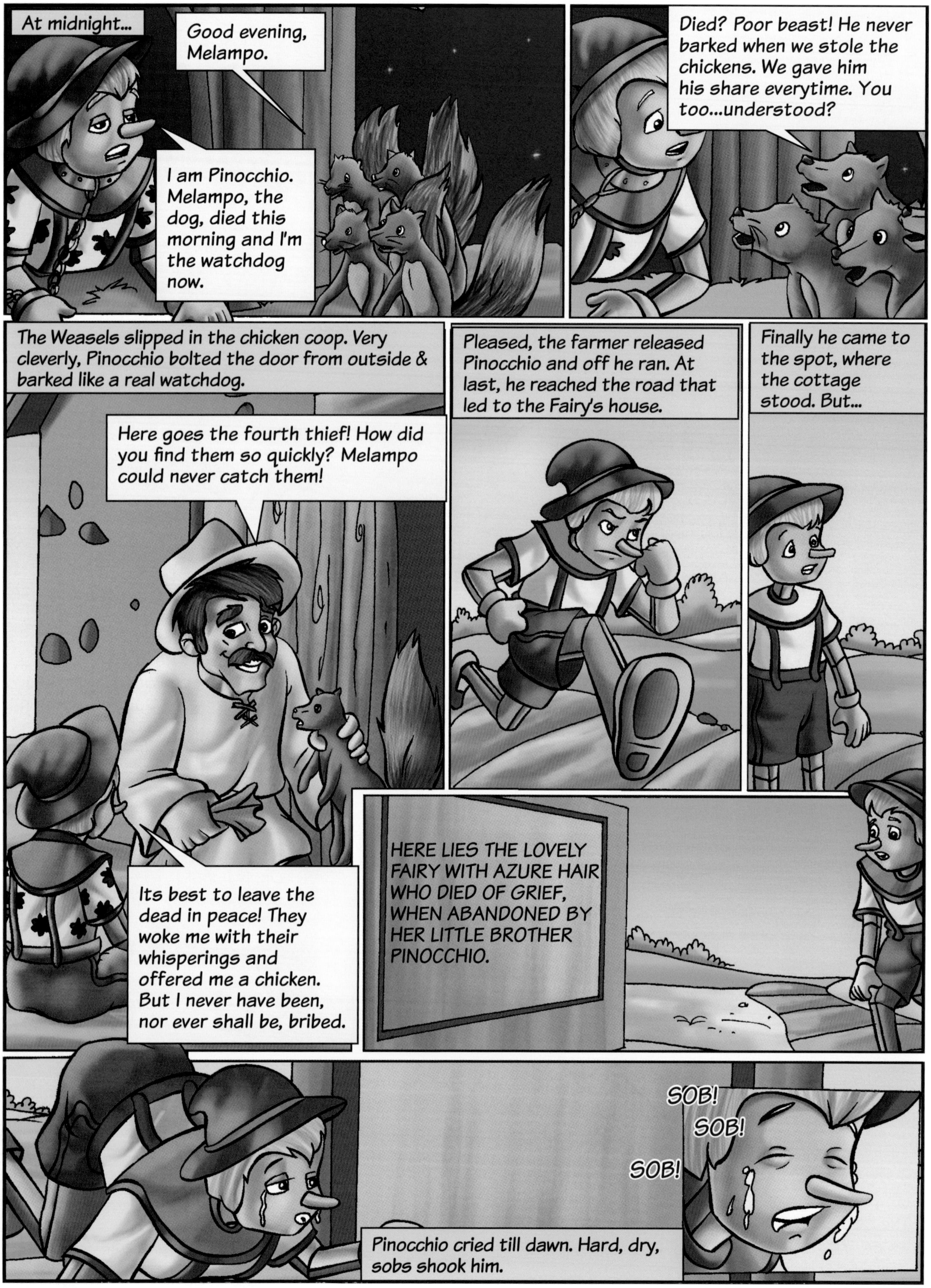
At midnight...
Good evening, Melampo.
I am Pinocchio. Melampo, the dog, died this morning and I'm the watchdog now.
Died? Poor beast! He never barked when we stole the chickens. We gave him his share everytime. You too...understood?
The Weasels slipped in the chicken coop. Very cleverly, Pinocchio bolted the door from outside & barked like a real watchdog.
Here goes the fourth thief! How did you find them so quickly? Melampo could never catch them!
Its best to leave the dead in peace! They woke me with their whisperings and offered me a chicken. But I never have been, nor ever shall be, bribed.
Pleased, the farmer released Pinocchio and off he ran. At last, he reached the road that led to the Fairy's house.
Finally he came to the spot, where the cottage stood. But...
HERE LIES THE LOVELY FAIRY WITH AZURE HAIR WHO DIED OF GRIEF, WHEN ABANDONED BY HER LITTLE BROTHER PINOCCHIO.
Pinocchio cried till dawn. Hard, dry, sobs shook him.
SOB!
SOB!
SOB!

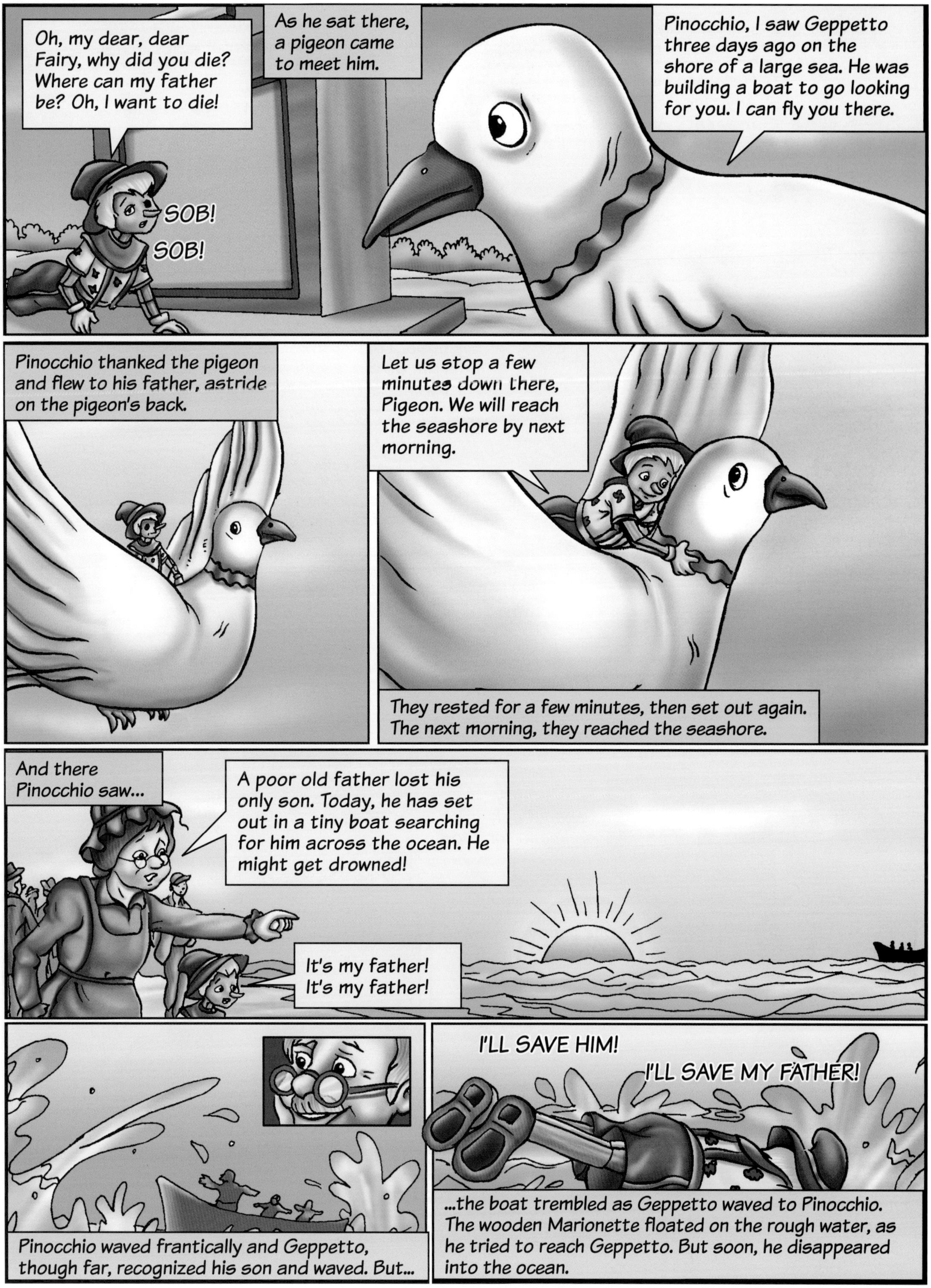
Oh, my dear, dear Fairy, why did you die? Where can my father be? Oh, I want to die!
SOB!
SOB!
As he sat there, a pigeon came to meet him.
Pinocchio, I saw Geppetto three days ago on the shore of a large sea. He was building a boat to go looking for you. I can fly you there.
Pinocchio thanked the pigeon and flew to his father, astride on the pigeon's back.
Let us stop a few minutes down there, Pigeon. We will reach the seashore by next morning.
They rested for a few minutes, then set out again. The next morning, they reached the seashore.
And there Pinocchio saw...
A poor old father lost his only son. Today, he has set out in a tiny boat searching for him across the ocean. He might get drowned!
It's my father! It's my father!
Pinocchio waved frantically and Geppetto, though far, recognized his son and waved. But...
I'LL SAVE HIM!
I'LL SAVE MY FATHER!
...the boat trembled as Geppetto waved to Pinocchio. The wooden Marionette floated on the rough water, as he tried to reach Geppetto. But soon, he disappeared into the ocean.

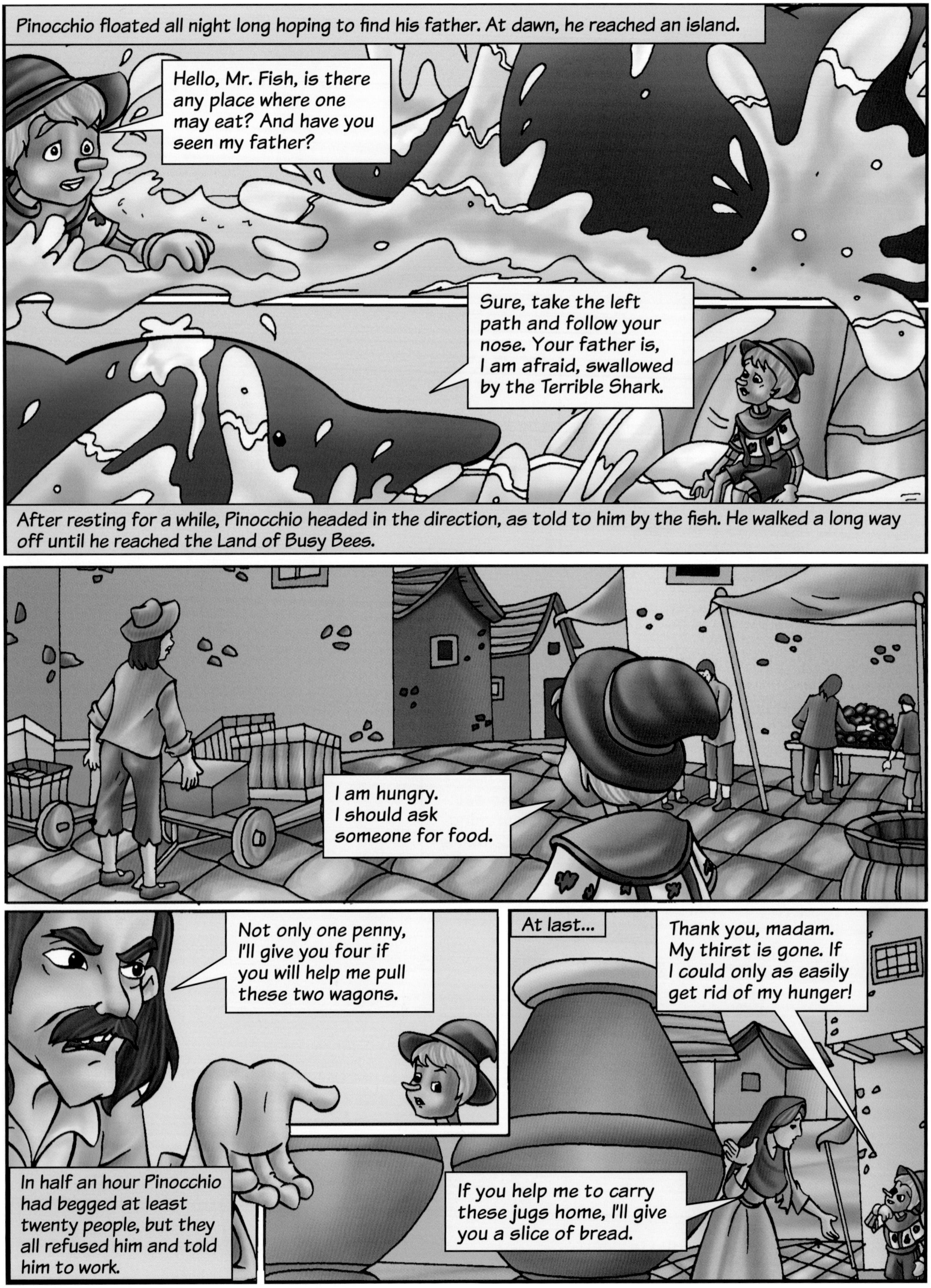
Pinocchio floated all night long hoping to find his father. At dawn, he reached an island.
Hello, Mr. Fish, is there any place where one may eat? And have you seen my father?
Sure, take the left path and follow your nose. Your father is, I am afraid, swallowed by the Terrible Shark.
After resting for a while, Pinocchio headed in the direction, as told to him by the fish. He walked a long way off until he reached the Land of Busy Bees.
I am hungry. I should ask someone for food.
Not only one penny, I'll give you four if you will help me pull these two wagons.
In half an hour Pinocchio had begged at least twenty people, but they all refused him and told him to work.
At last...
Thank you, madam. My thirst is gone. If I could only as easily get rid of my hunger!
If you help me to carry these jugs home, I'll give you a slice of bread.

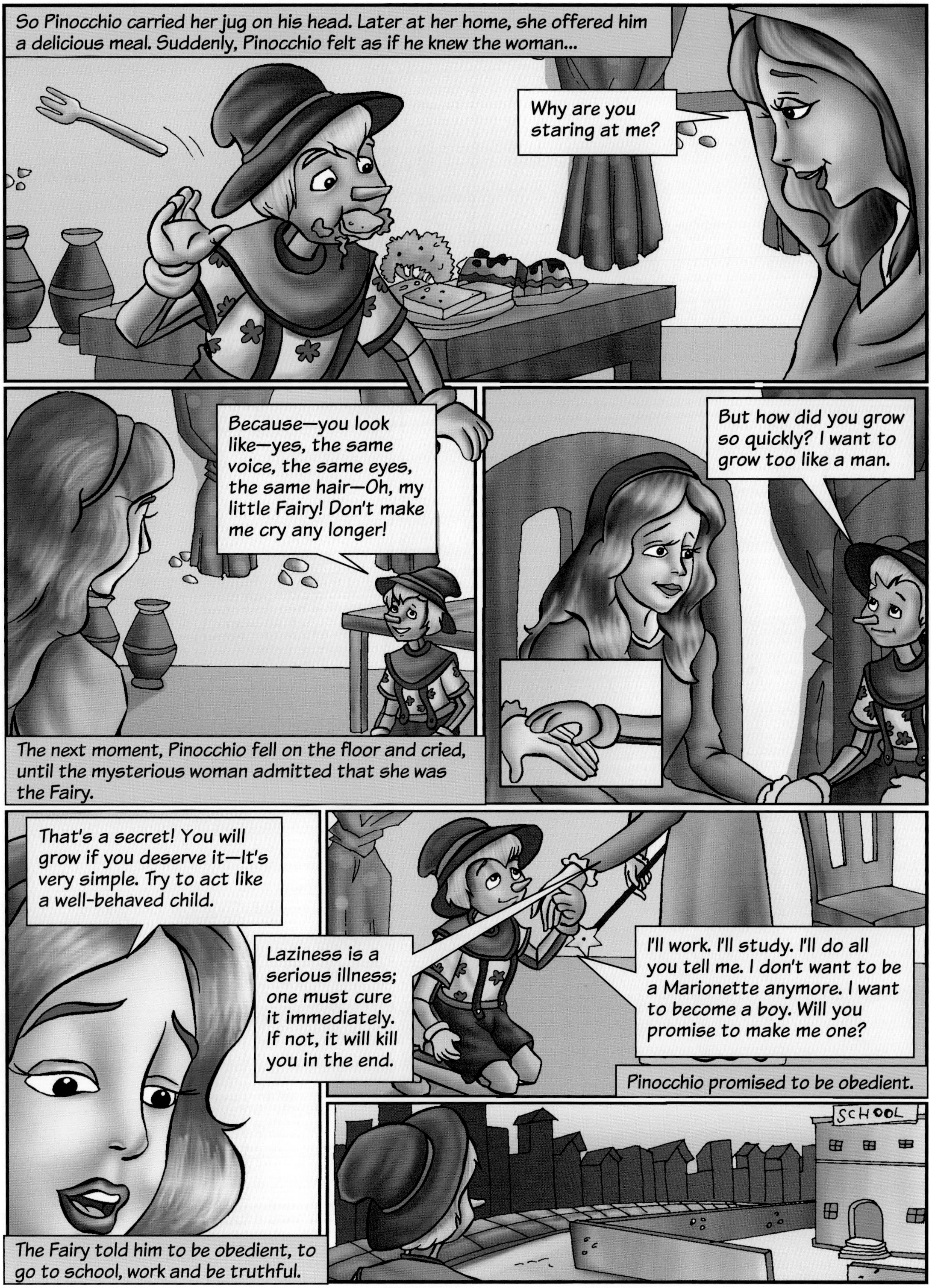
So Pinocchio carried her jug on his head. Later at her home, she offered him a delicious meal. Suddenly, Pinocchio felt as if he knew the woman...
Why are you staring at me?
Because—you look like—yes, the same voice, the same eyes, the same hair—Oh, my little Fairy! Don't make me cry any longer!
The next moment, Pinocchio fell on the floor and cried, until the mysterious woman admitted that she was the Fairy.
But how did you grow so quickly? I want to grow too like a man.
That's a secret! You will grow if you deserve it—It's very simple. Try to act like a well-behaved child.
Laziness is a serious illness; one must cure it immediately. If not, it will kill you in the end.
I'll work. I'll study. I'll do all you tell me. I don't want to be a Marionette anymore. I want to become a boy. Will you promise to make me one?
Pinocchio promised to be obedient.
SCHOOL
The Fairy told him to be obedient, to go to school, work and be truthful.

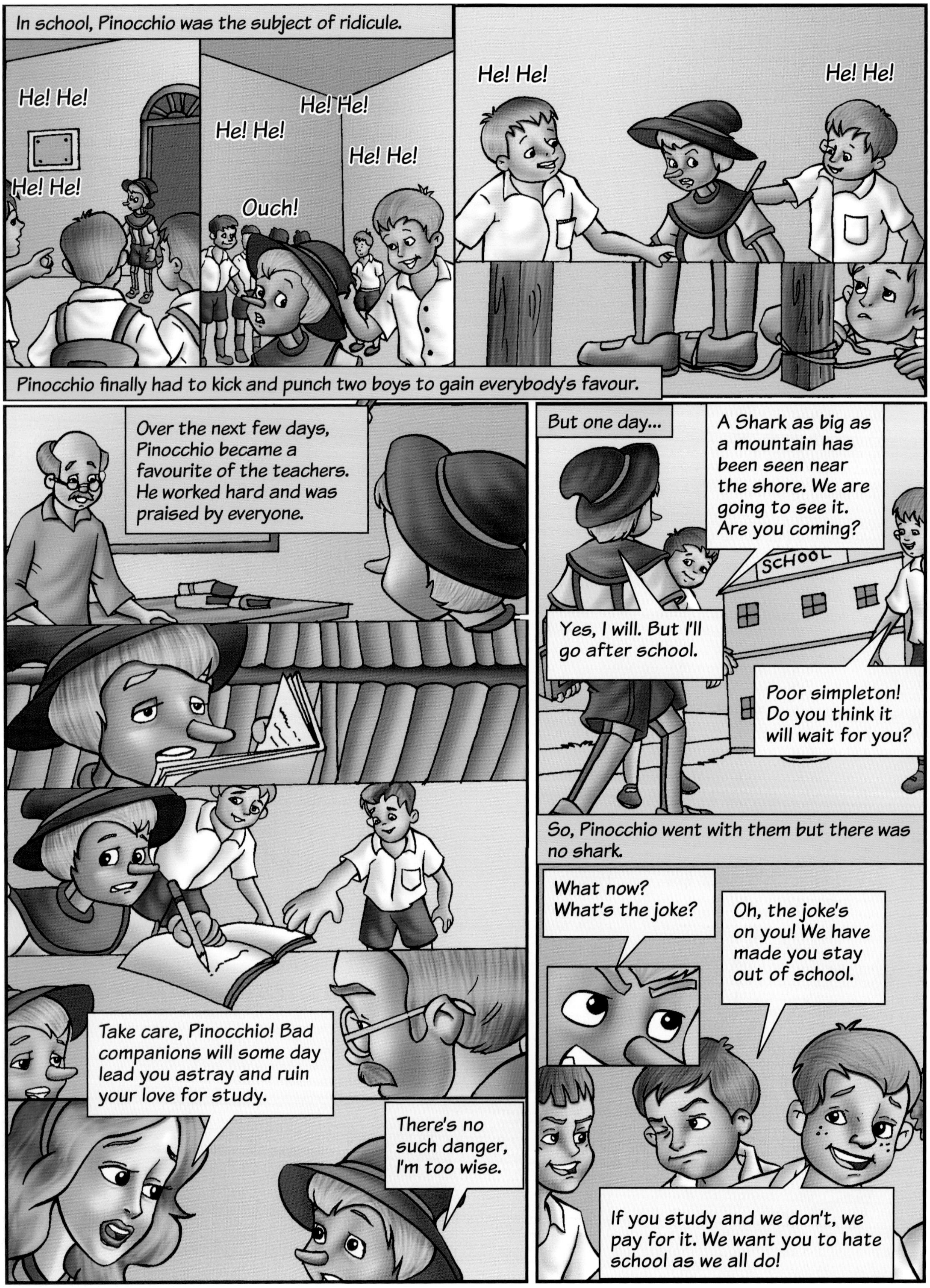
In school, Pinocchio was the subject of ridicule.
He! He!
He! He!
He! He!
He! He!
He! He!
Ouch!
He! He!
He! He!
Pinocchio finally had to kick and punch two boys to gain everybody's favour.
Over the next few days, Pinocchio became a favourite of the teachers. He worked hard and was praised by everyone.
Take care, Pinocchio! Bad companions will some day lead you astray and ruin your love for study.
There's no such danger, I'm too wise.
But one day...
A Shark as big as a mountain has been seen near the shore. We are going to see it. Are you coming?
SCHOOL
Yes, I will. But I'll go after school.
Poor simpleton! Do you think it will wait for you?
So, Pinocchio went with them but there was no shark.
What now? What's the joke?
Oh, the joke's on you! We have made you stay out of school.
If you study and we don't, we pay for it. We want you to hate school as we all do!

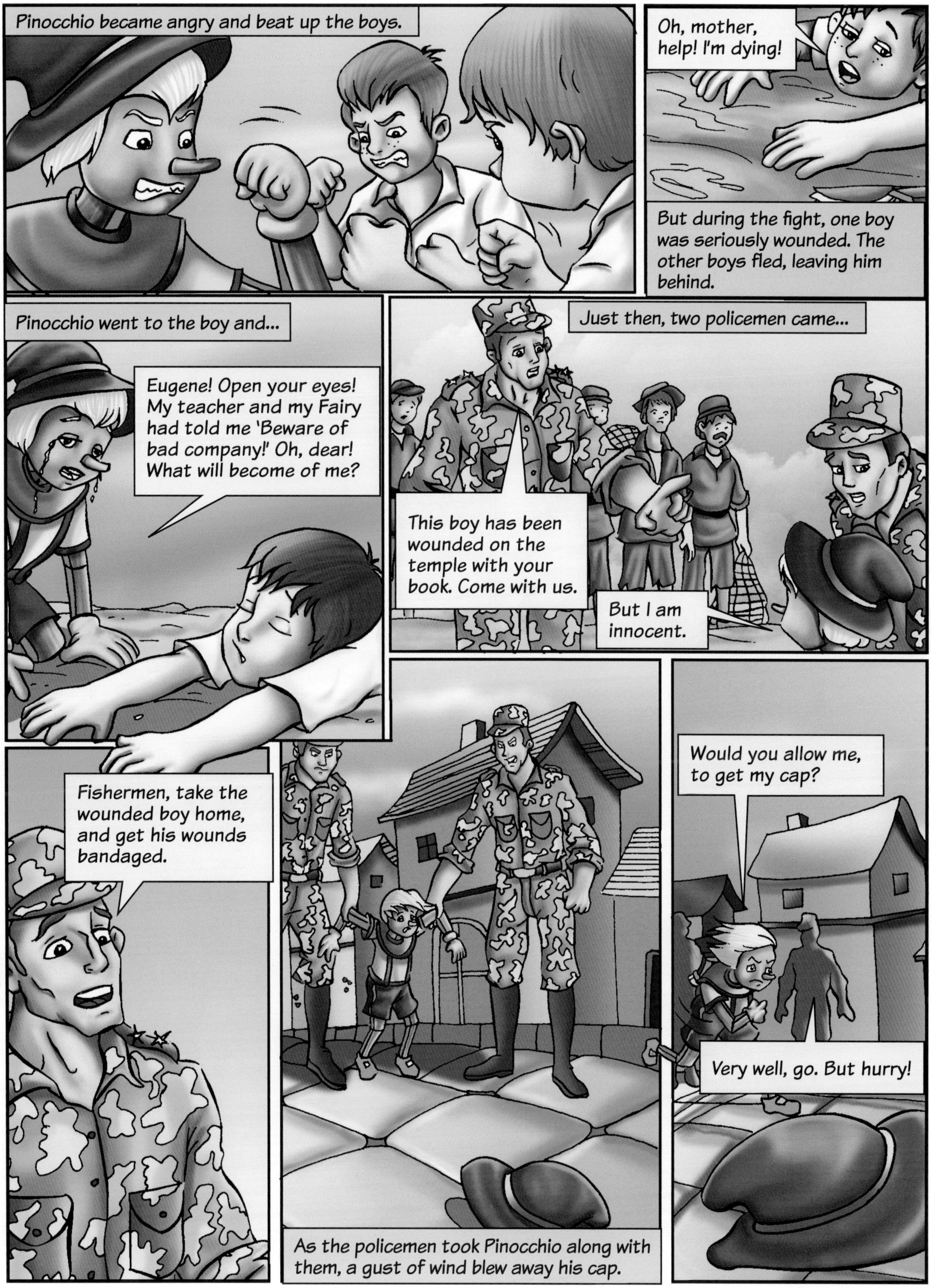
Pinocchio became angry and beat up the boys.
Oh, mother, help! I'm dying!
But during the fight, one boy was seriously wounded. The other boys fled, leaving him behind.
Pinocchio went to the boy and...
Eugene! Open your eyes! My teacher and my Fairy had told me 'Beware of bad company!' Oh, dear! What will become of me?
Just then, two policemen came...
This boy has been wounded on the temple with your book. Come with us.
But I am innocent.
Fishermen, take the wounded boy home, and get his wounds bandaged.
As the policemen took Pinocchio along with them, a gust of wind blew away his cap.
Would you allow me, to get my cap?
Very well, go. But hurry!

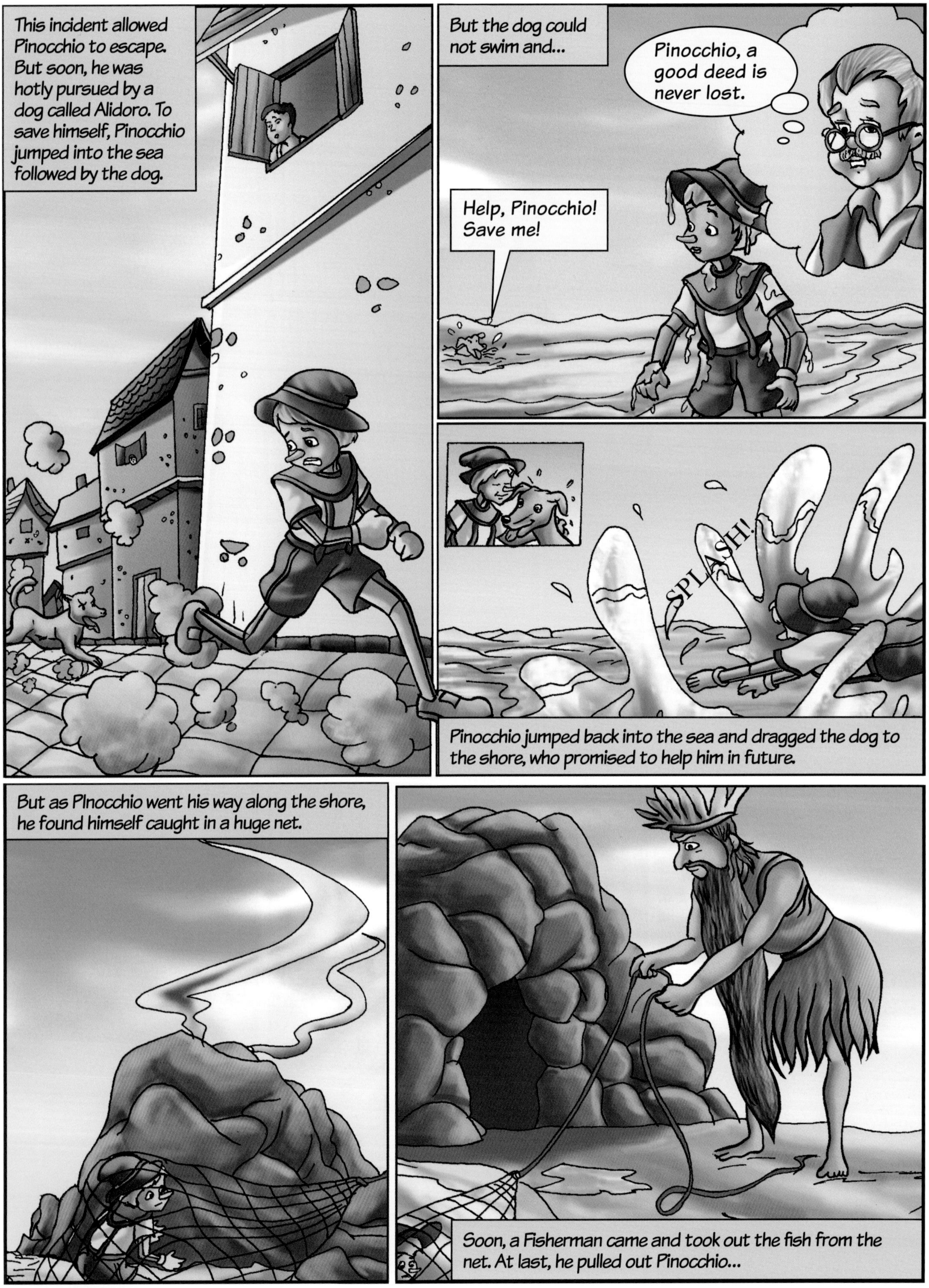
This incident allowed Pinocchio to escape. But soon, he was hotly pursued by a dog called Alidoro. To save himself, Pinocchio jumped into the sea followed by the dog.
But the dog could not swim and...
Help, Pinocchio! Save me!
Pinocchio, a good deed is never lost.
SPLASH!
Pinocchio jumped back into the sea and dragged the dog to the shore, who promised to help him in future.
But as Pinocchio went his way along the shore, he found himself caught in a huge net.
Soon, a Fisherman came and took out the fish from the net. At last, he pulled out Pinocchio...

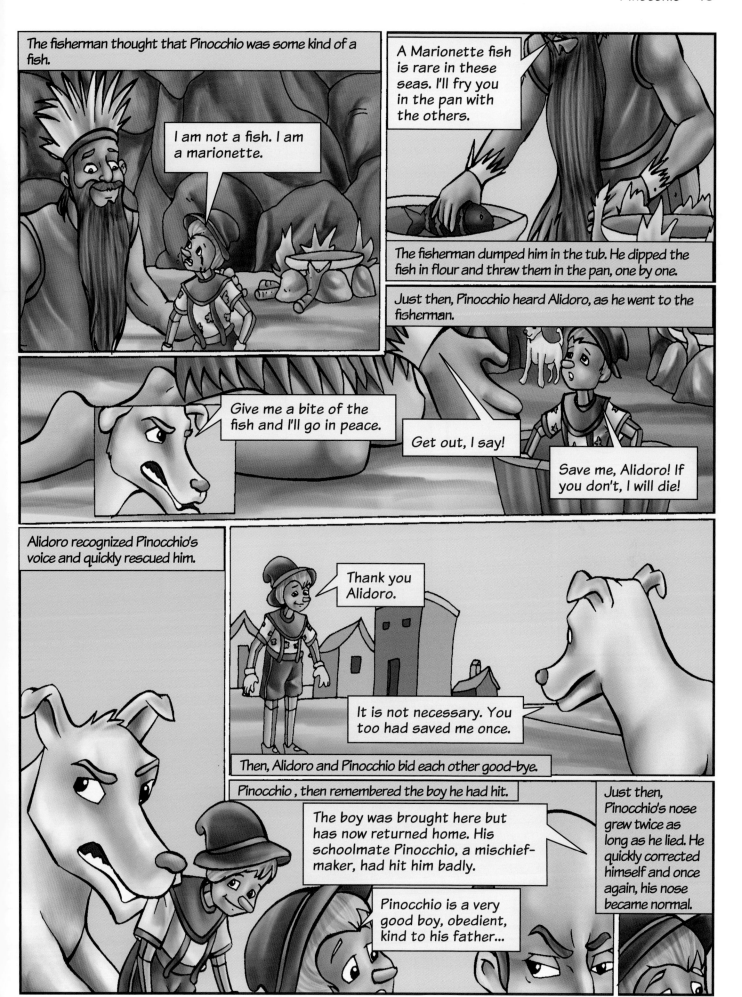

The fisherman thought that Pinocchio was some kind of a fish.

I am not a fish. I am a marionette.

A Marionette fish is rare in these seas. I'll fry you in the pan with the others.

The fisherman dumped him in the tub. He dipped the fish in flour and threw them in the pan, one by one.

Just then, Pinocchio heard Alidoro, as he went to the fisherman.

Give me a bite of the fish and I'll go in peace.

Get out, I say!

Save me, Alidoro! If you don't, I will die!

Alidoro recognized Pinocchio's voice and quickly rescued him.

Thank you Alidoro.

It is not necessary. You too had saved me once.

Then, Alidoro and Pinocchio bid each other good-bye.

Pinocchio, then remembered the boy he had hit.

The boy was brought here but has now returned home. His schoolmate Pinocchio, a mischief-maker, had hit him badly.

Pinocchio is a very good boy, obedient, kind to his father...

Just then, Pinocchio's nose grew twice as long as he lied. He quickly corrected himself and once again, his nose became normal.

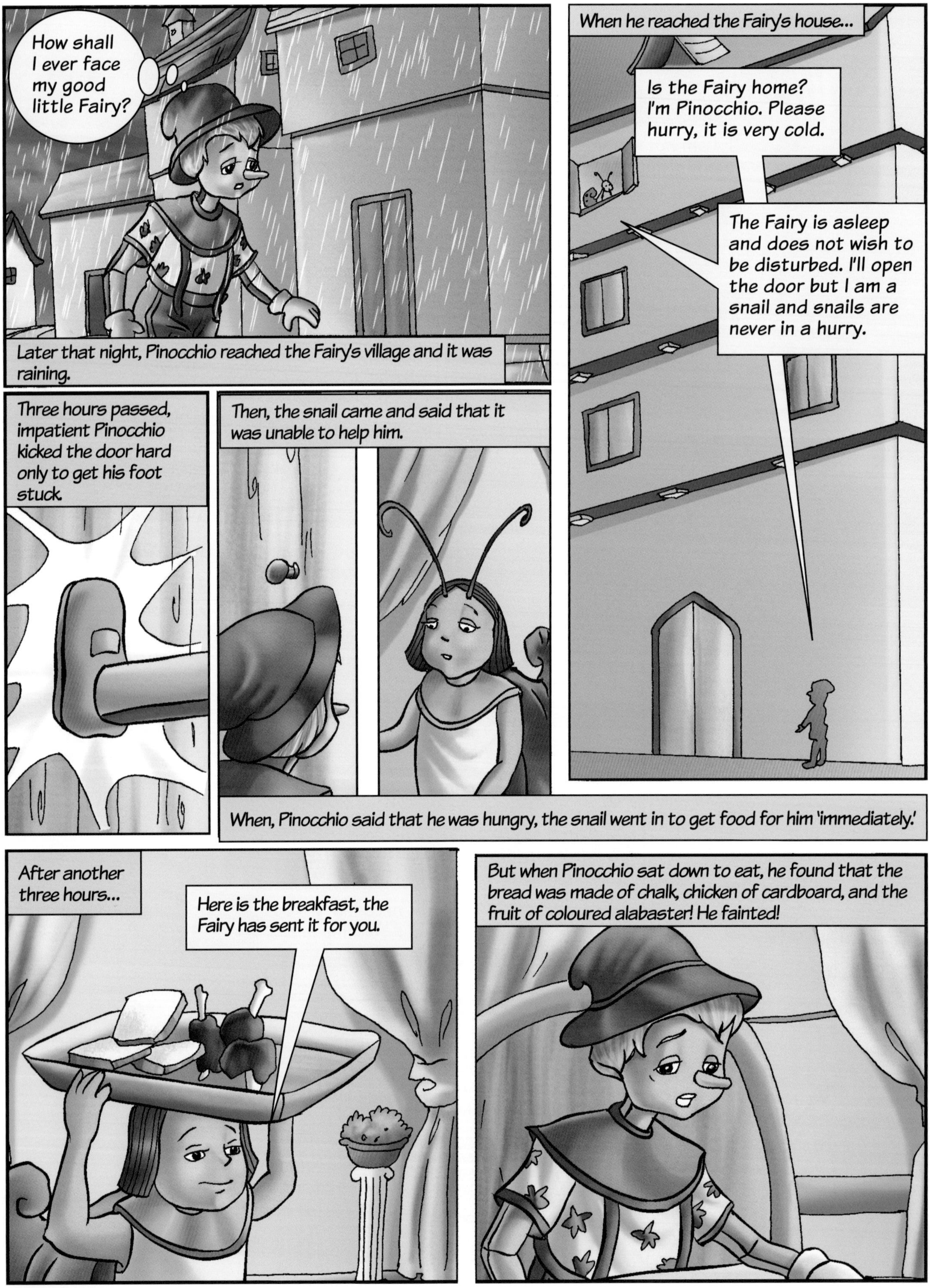
How shall I ever face my good little Fairy?
Later that night, Pinocchio reached the Fairy's village and it was raining.
When he reached the Fairy's house...
Is the Fairy home? I'm Pinocchio. Please hurry, it is very cold.
The Fairy is asleep and does not wish to be disturbed. I'll open the door but I am a snail and snails are never in a hurry.
Three hours passed, impatient Pinocchio kicked the door hard only to get his foot stuck.
Then, the snail came and said that it was unable to help him.
When, Pinocchio said that he was hungry, the snail went in to get food for him 'immediately.'
After another three hours...
Here is the breakfast, the Fairy has sent it for you.
But when Pinocchio sat down to eat, he found that the bread was made of chalk, chicken of cardboard, and the fruit of coloured alabaster! He fainted!

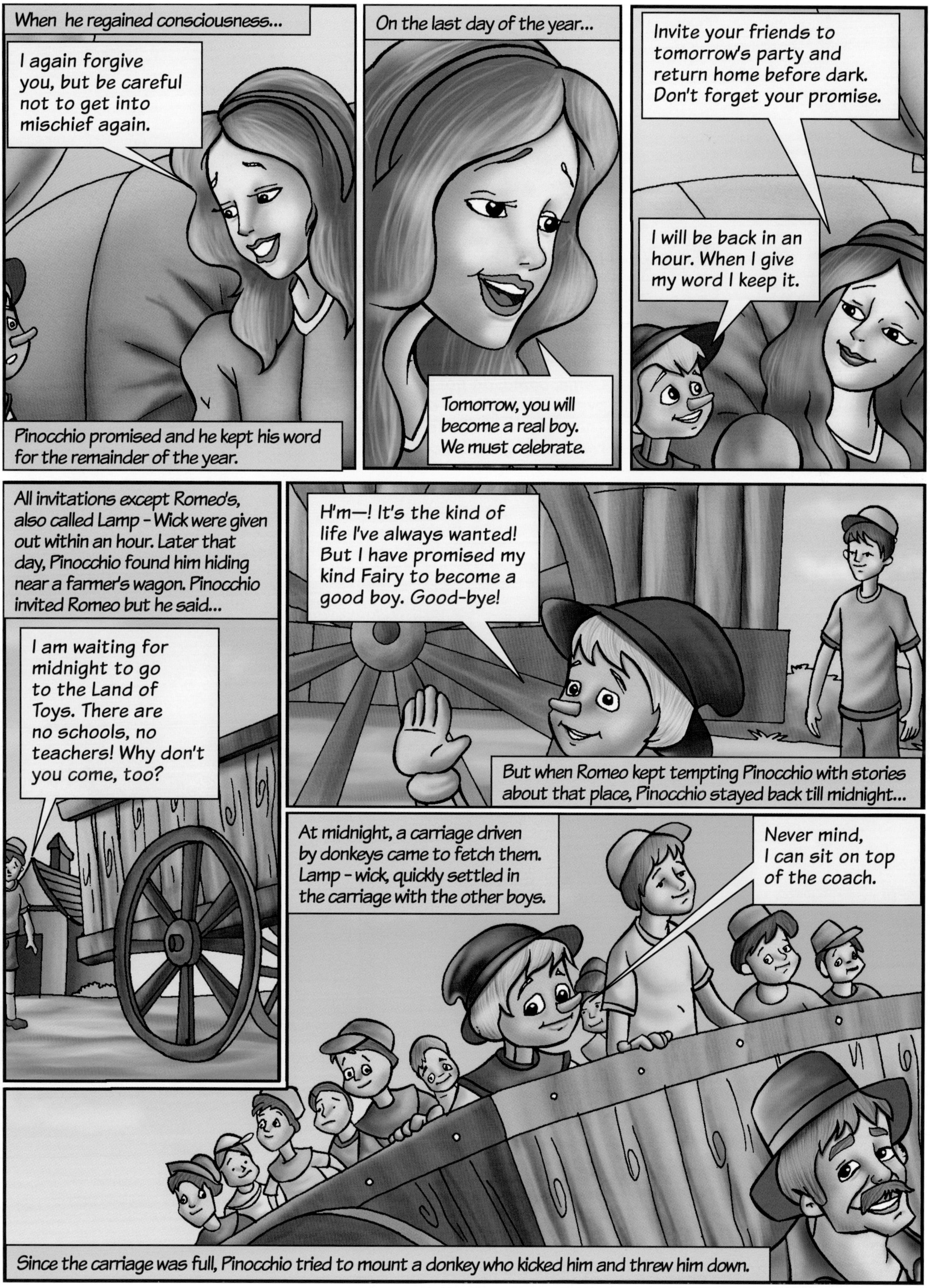
When he regained consciousness...
I again forgive you, but be careful not to get into mischief again.
Pinocchio promised and he kept his word for the remainder of the year.
On the last day of the year...
Tomorrow, you will become a real boy. We must celebrate.
Invite your friends to tomorrow's party and return home before dark. Don't forget your promise.
I will be back in an hour. When I give my word I keep it.
All invitations except Romeo's, also called Lamp - Wick were given out within an hour. Later that day, Pinocchio found him hiding near a farmer's wagon. Pinocchio invited Romeo but he said...
I am waiting for midnight to go to the Land of Toys. There are no schools, no teachers! Why don't you come, too?
H'm—! It's the kind of life I've always wanted! But I have promised my kind Fairy to become a good boy. Good-bye!
But when Romeo kept tempting Pinocchio with stories about that place, Pinocchio stayed back till midnight...
At midnight, a carriage driven by donkeys came to fetch them. Lamp - wick, quickly settled in the carriage with the other boys.
Never mind, I can sit on top of the coach.
Since the carriage was full, Pinocchio tried to mount a donkey who kicked him and threw him down.

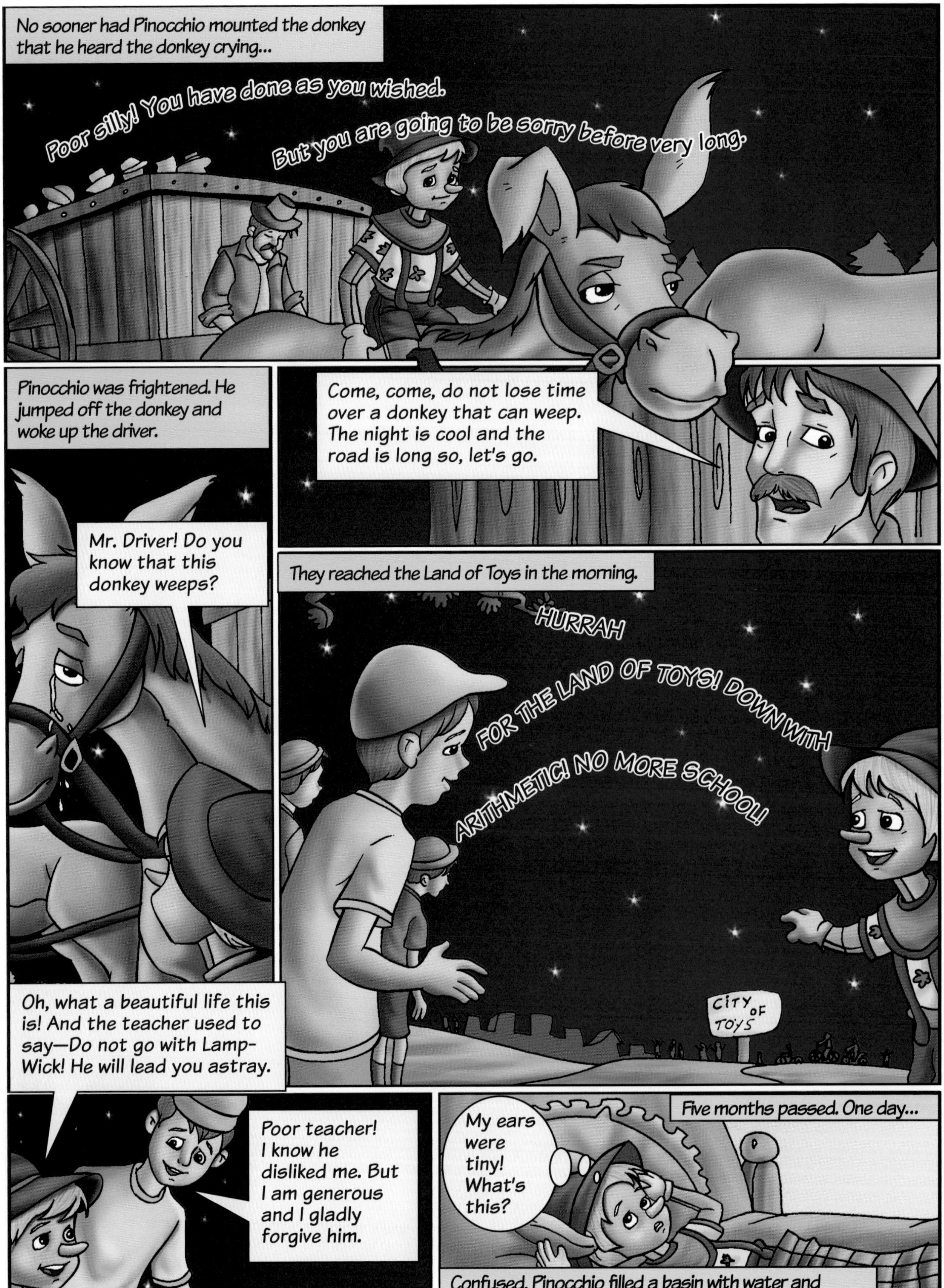
No sooner had Pinocchio mounted the donkey that he heard the donkey crying...
Poor silly! You have done as you wished.
But you are going to be sorry before very long.
Pinocchio was frightened. He jumped off the donkey and woke up the driver.
Mr. Driver! Do you know that this donkey weeps?
Come, come, do not lose time over a donkey that can weep. The night is cool and the road is long so, let's go.
They reached the Land of Toys in the morning.
HURRAH
FOR THE LAND OF TOYS! DOWN WITH
ARITHMETIC! NO MORE SCHOOL!
CITY OF TOYS
Oh, what a beautiful life this is! And the teacher used to say—Do not go with Lamp-Wick! He will lead you astray.
Poor teacher! I know he disliked me. But I am generous and I gladly forgive him.
Five months passed. One day...
My ears were tiny! What's this?
Confused, Pinocchio filled a basin with water and

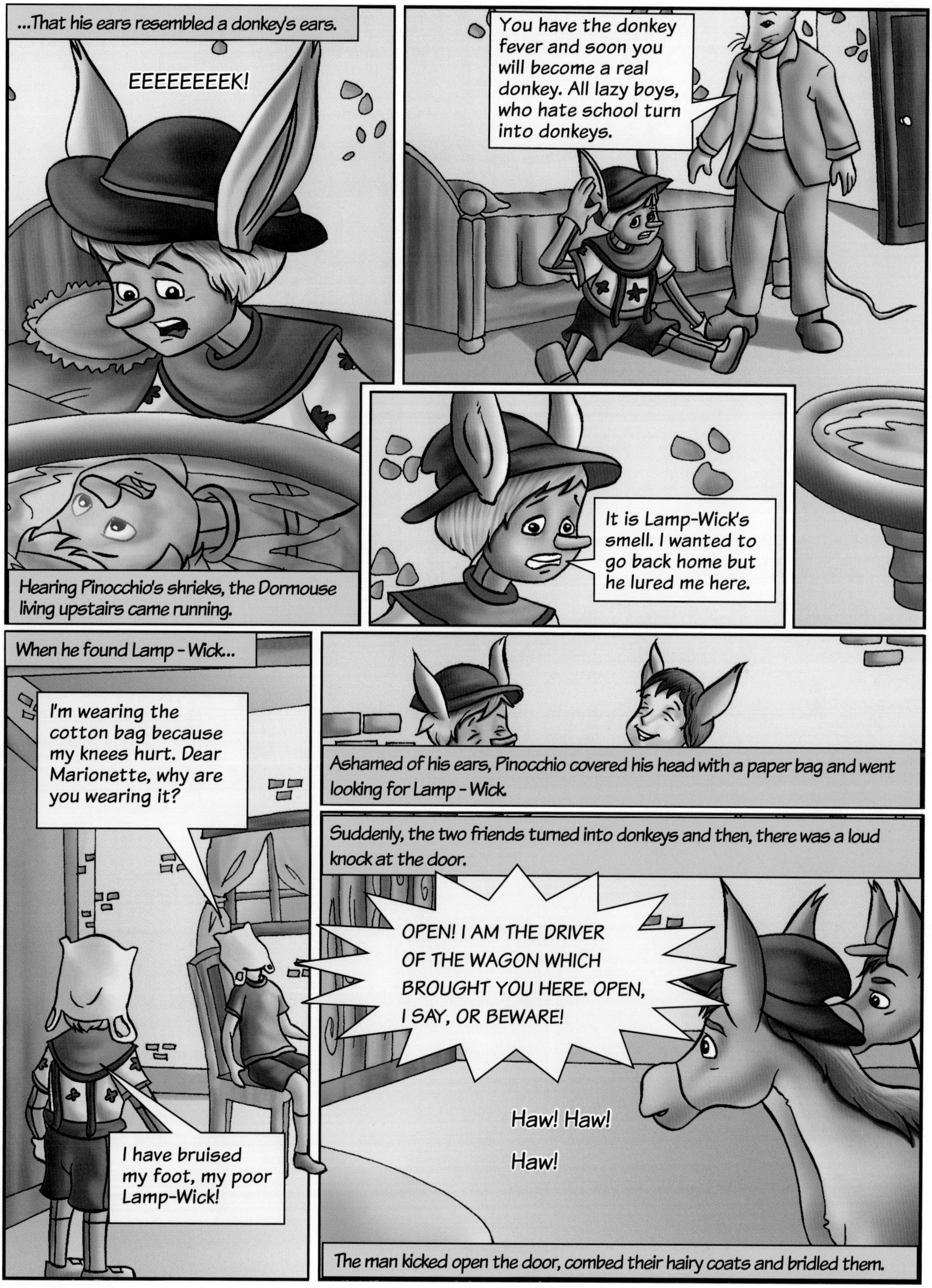
...That his ears resembled a donkey's ears.
EEEEEEEEK!
Hearing Pinocchio's shrieks, the Dormouse living upstairs came running.
You have the donkey fever and soon you will become a real donkey. All lazy boys, who hate school turn into donkeys.
It is Lamp-Wick's smell. I wanted to go back home but he lured me here.
When he found Lamp - Wick...
Ashamed of his ears, Pinocchio covered his head with a paper bag and went looking for Lamp - Wick.
I'm wearing the cotton bag because my knees hurt. Dear Marionette, why are you wearing it?
I have bruised my foot, my poor Lamp-Wick!
Suddenly, the two friends turned into donkeys and then, there was a loud knock at the door.
OPEN! I AM THE DRIVER OF THE WAGON WHICH BROUGHT YOU HERE. OPEN, I SAY, OR BEWARE!
Haw! Haw!
Haw!
The man kicked open the door, combed their hairy coats and bridled them.

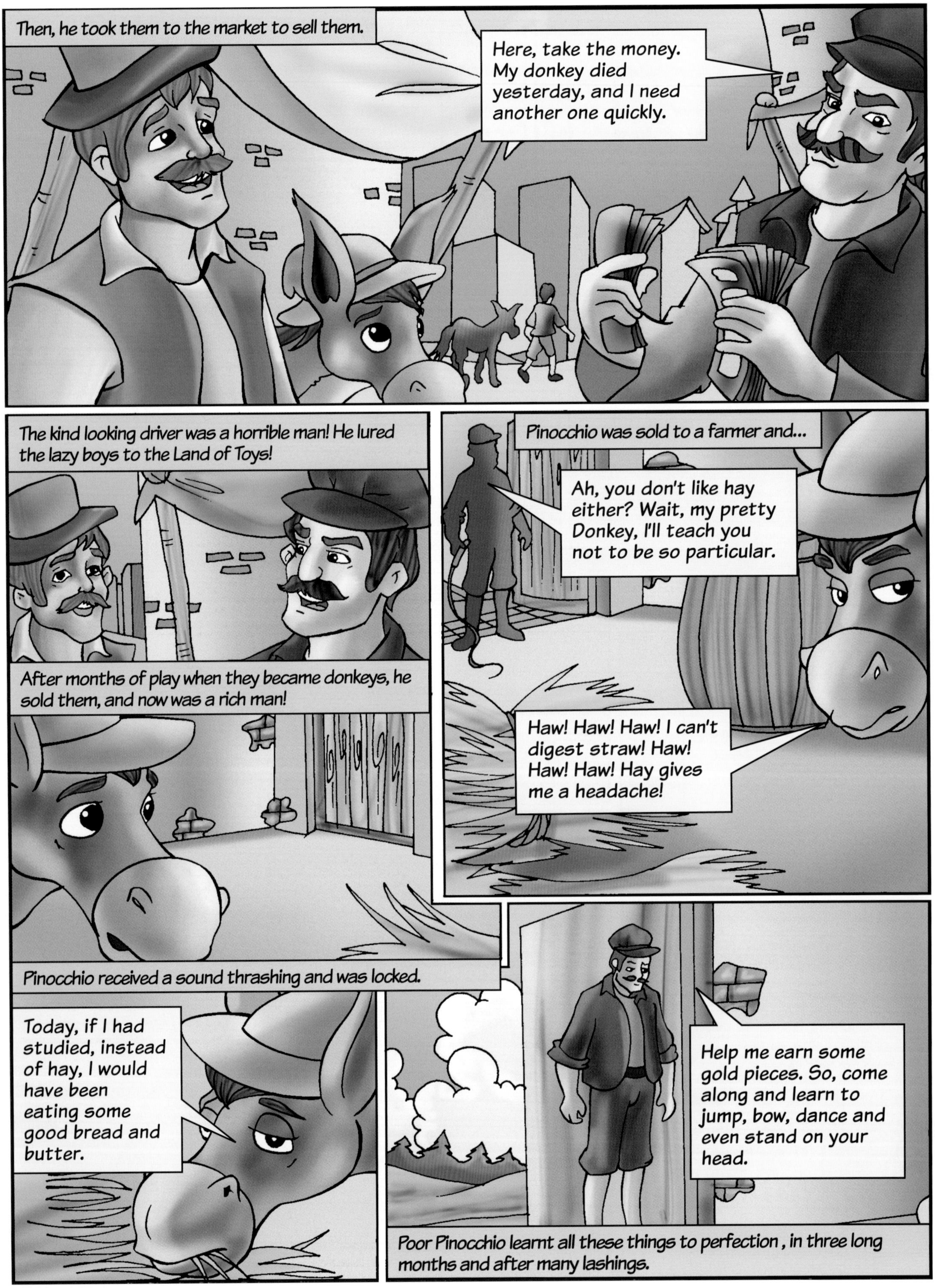
Then, he took them to the market to sell them.
Here, take the money. My donkey died yesterday, and I need another one quickly.
The kind looking driver was a horrible man! He lured the lazy boys to the Land of Toys!
After months of play when they became donkeys, he sold them, and now was a rich man!
Pinocchio was sold to a farmer and...
Ah, you don't like hay either? Wait, my pretty Donkey, I'll teach you not to be so particular.
Haw! Haw! Haw! I can't digest straw! Haw! Haw! Haw! Hay gives me a headache!
Pinocchio received a sound thrashing and was locked.
Today, if I had studied, instead of hay, I would have been eating some good bread and butter.
Help me earn some gold pieces. So, come along and learn to jump, bow, dance and even stand on your head.
Poor Pinocchio learnt all these things to perfection , in three long months and after many lashings.

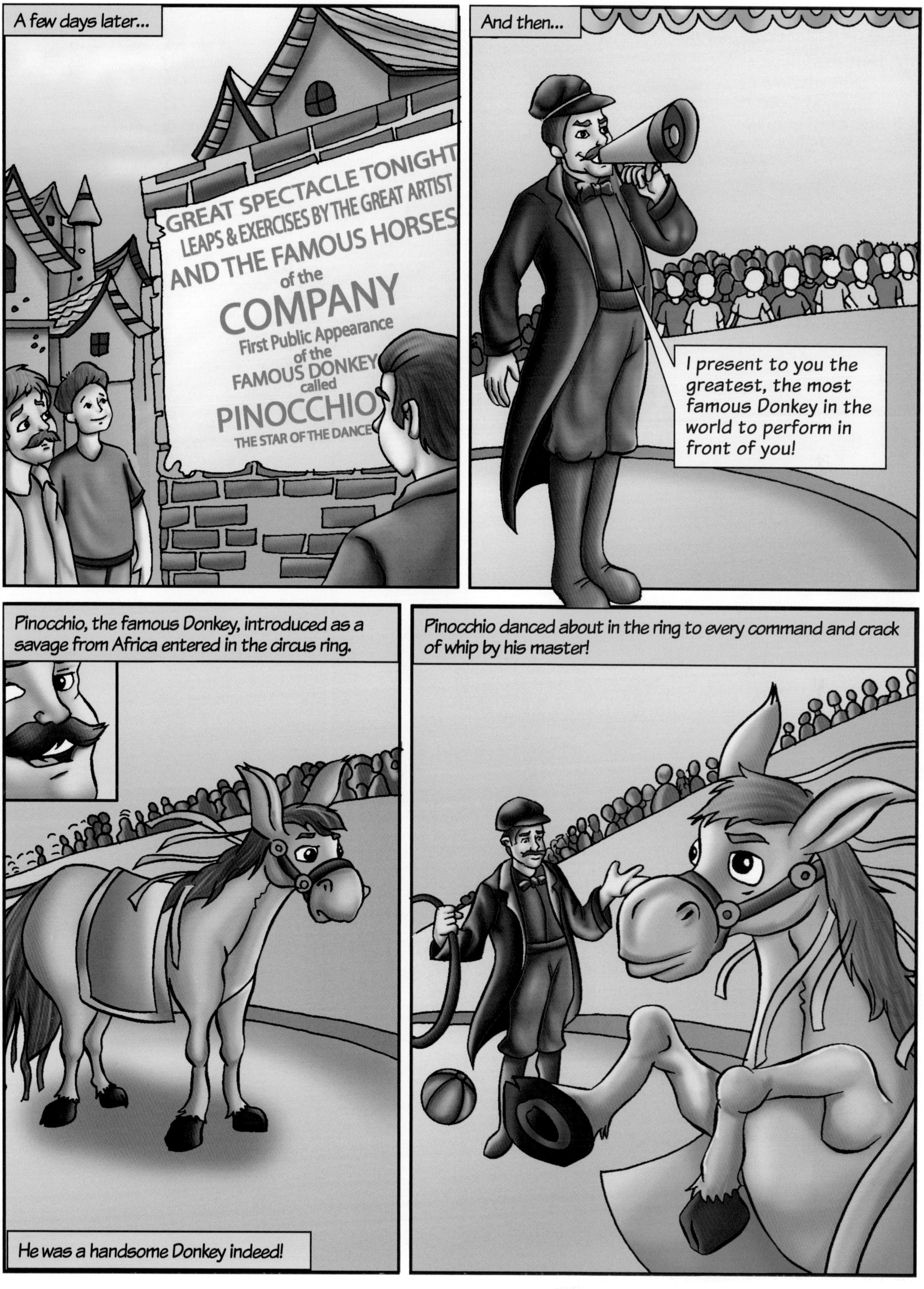
A few days later...
GREAT SPECTACLE TONIGHT
LEAPS & EXERCISES BY THE GREAT ARTIST
AND THE FAMOUS HORSES
of the
COMPANY
First Public Appearance
of the
FAMOUS DONKEY
called
PINOCCHIO
THE STAR OF THE DANCE
And then...
I present to you the greatest, the most famous Donkey in the world to perform in front of you!
Pinocchio, the famous Donkey, introduced as a savage from Africa entered in the circus ring.
He was a handsome Donkey indeed!
Pinocchio danced about in the ring to every command and crack of whip by his master!

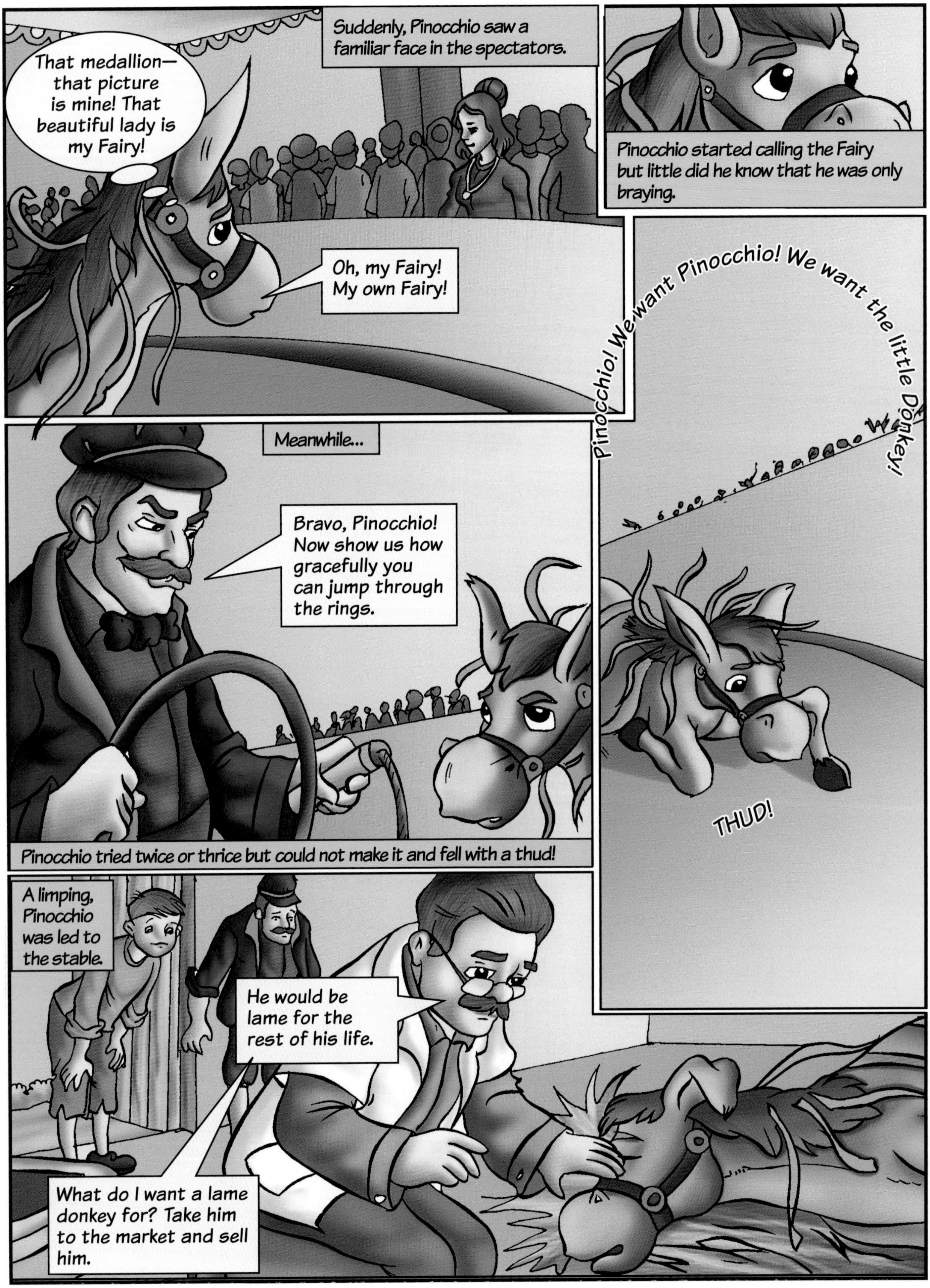
Suddenly, Pinocchio saw a familiar face in the spectators.
That medallion—that picture is mine! That beautiful lady is my Fairy!
Oh, my Fairy! My own Fairy!
Pinocchio started calling the Fairy but little did he know that he was only braying.
Pinocchio! We want Pinocchio! We want the little Donkey!
Meanwhile...
Bravo, Pinocchio! Now show us how gracefully you can jump through the rings.
Pinocchio tried twice or thrice but could not make it and fell with a thud!
THUD!
A limping, Pinocchio was led to the stable.
He would be lame for the rest of his life.
What do I want a lame donkey for? Take him to the market and sell him.

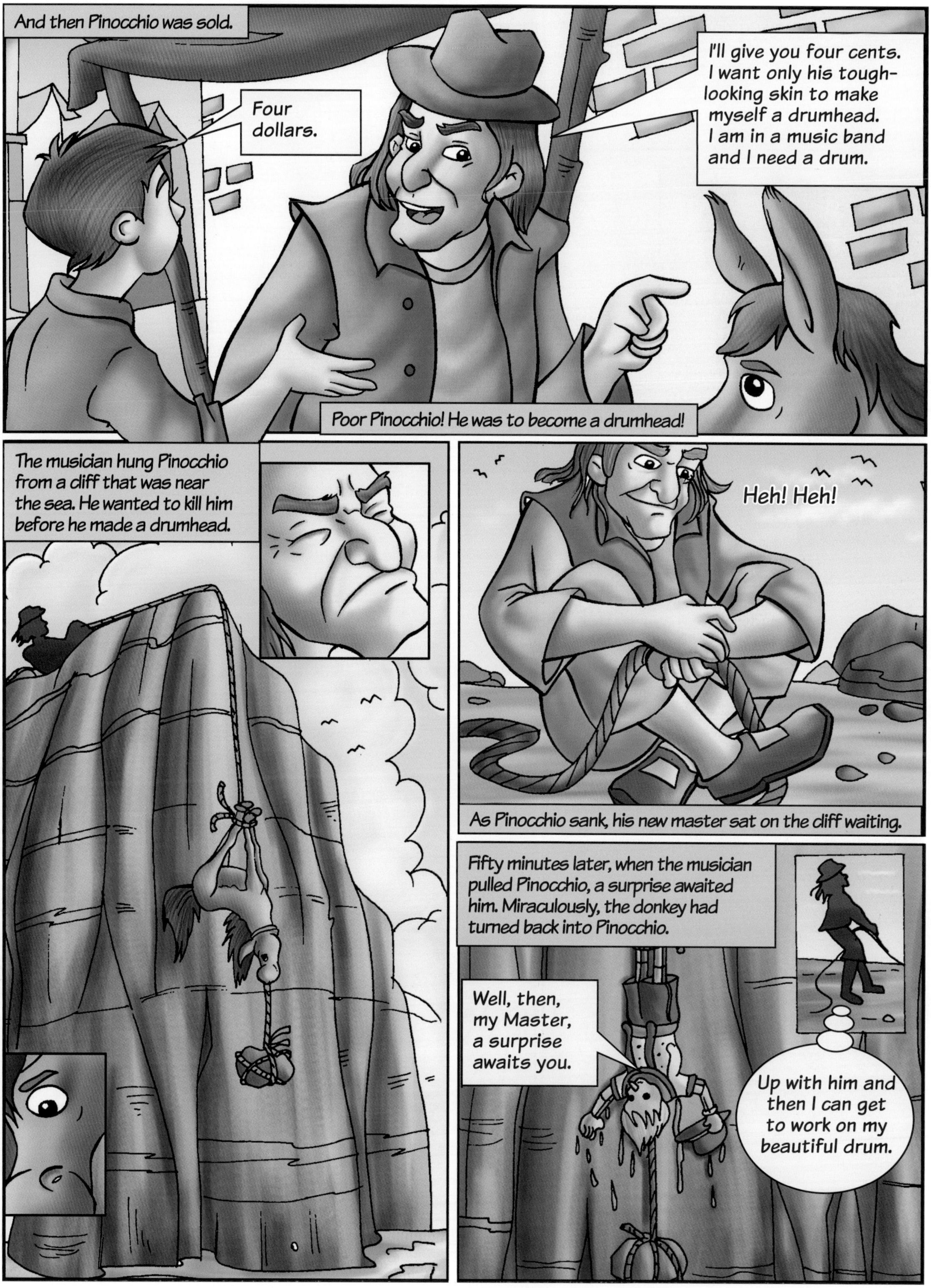
And then Pinocchio was sold.
Four dollars.
I'll give you four cents. I want only his tough-looking skin to make myself a drumhead. I am in a music band and I need a drum.
Poor Pinocchio! He was to become a drumhead!
The musician hung Pinocchio from a cliff that was near the sea. He wanted to kill him before he made a drumhead.
Heh! Heh!
As Pinocchio sank, his new master sat on the cliff waiting.
Fifty minutes later, when the musician pulled Pinocchio, a surprise awaited him. Miraculously, the donkey had turned back into Pinocchio.
Well, then, my Master, a surprise awaits you.
Up with him and then I can get to work on my beautiful drum.

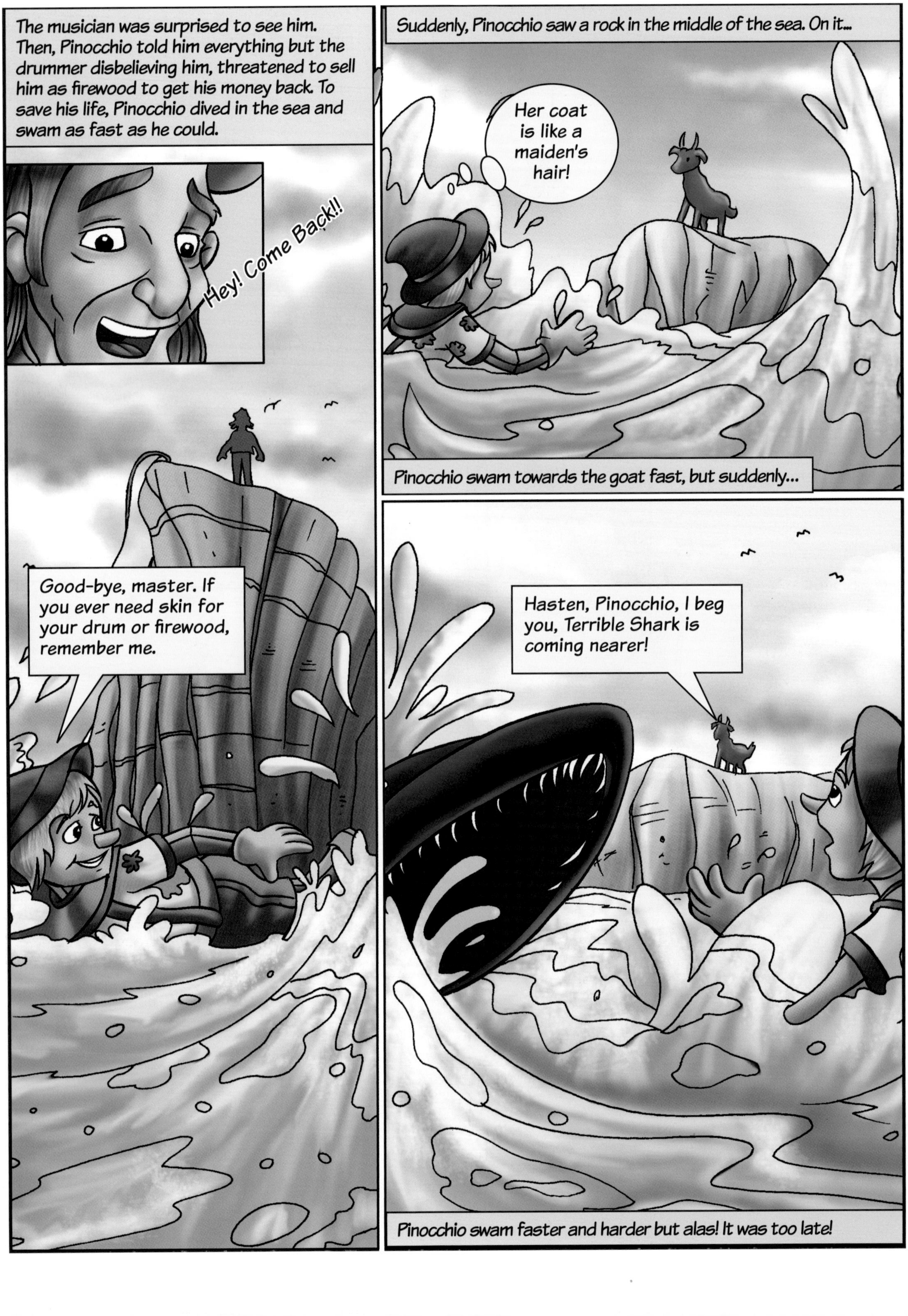
The musician was surprised to see him. Then, Pinocchio told him everything but the drummer disbelieving him, threatened to sell him as firewood to get his money back. To save his life, Pinocchio dived in the sea and swam as fast as he could.
Hey! Come Back!!
Good-bye, master. If you ever need skin for your drum or firewood, remember me.
Suddenly, Pinocchio saw a rock in the middle of the sea. On it...
Her coat is like a maiden's hair!
Pinocchio swam towards the goat fast, but suddenly...
Hasten, Pinocchio, I beg you, Terrible Shark is coming nearer!
Pinocchio swam faster and harder but alas! It was too late!

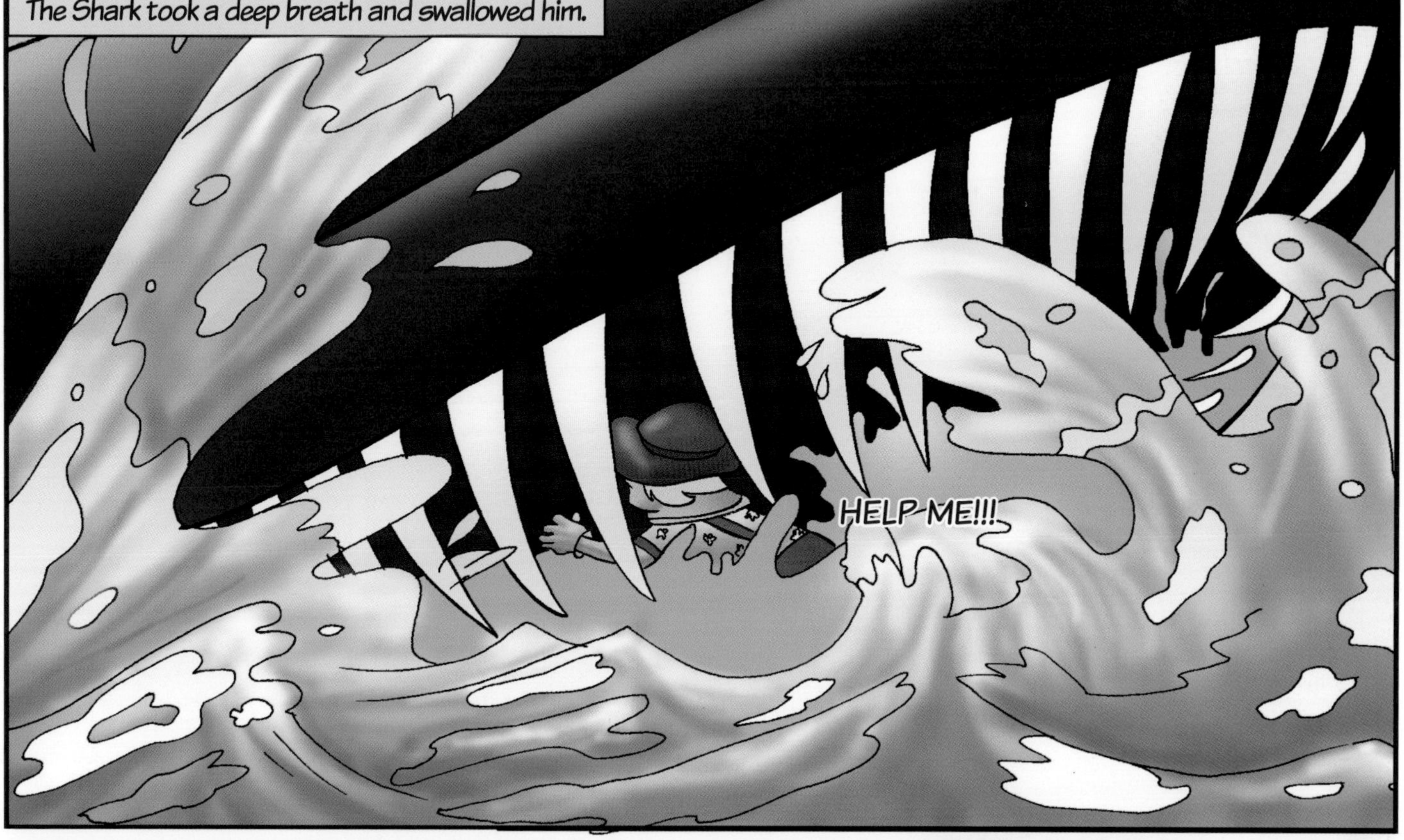
The Shark took a deep breath and swallowed him.
HELP ME!!!

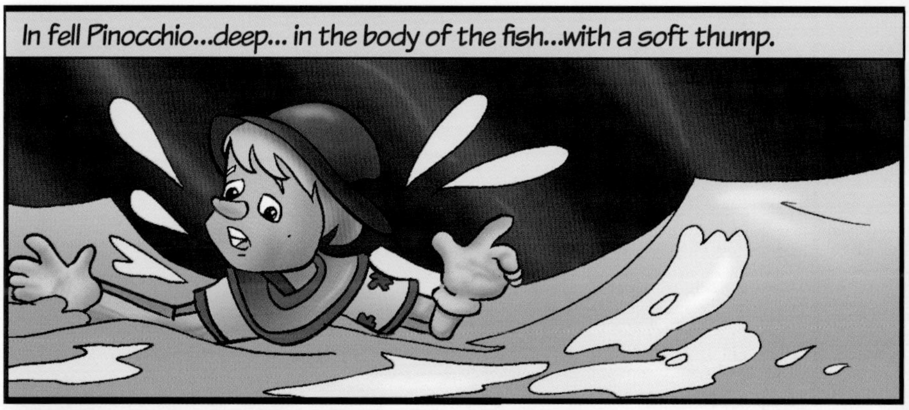
In fell Pinocchio...deep... in the body of the fish...with a soft thump.

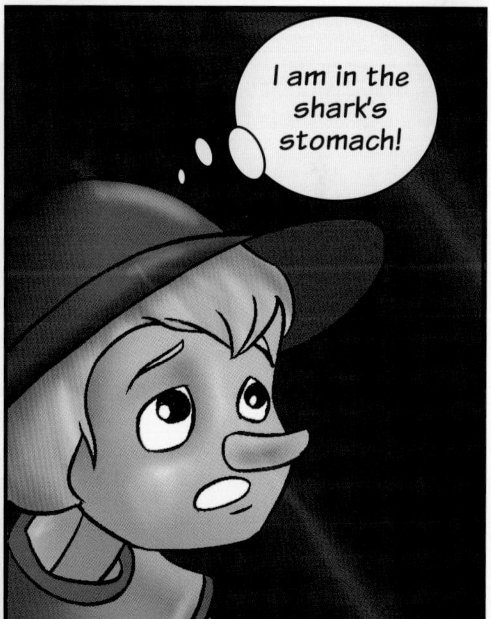
I am in the shark's stomach!

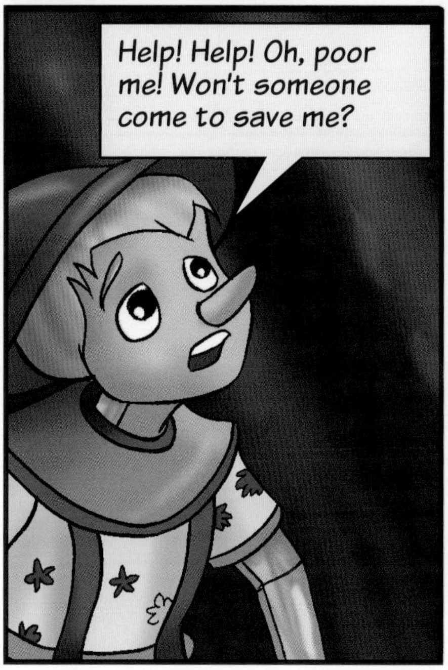
Help! Help! Oh, poor me! Won't someone come to save me?

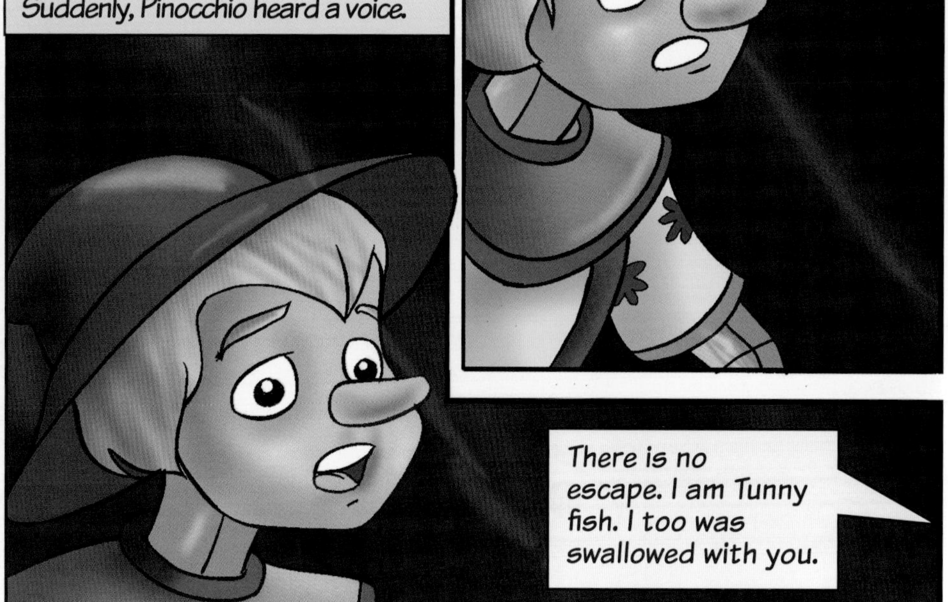
Suddenly, Pinocchio heard a voice.
There is no escape. I am Tunny fish. I too was swallowed with you.

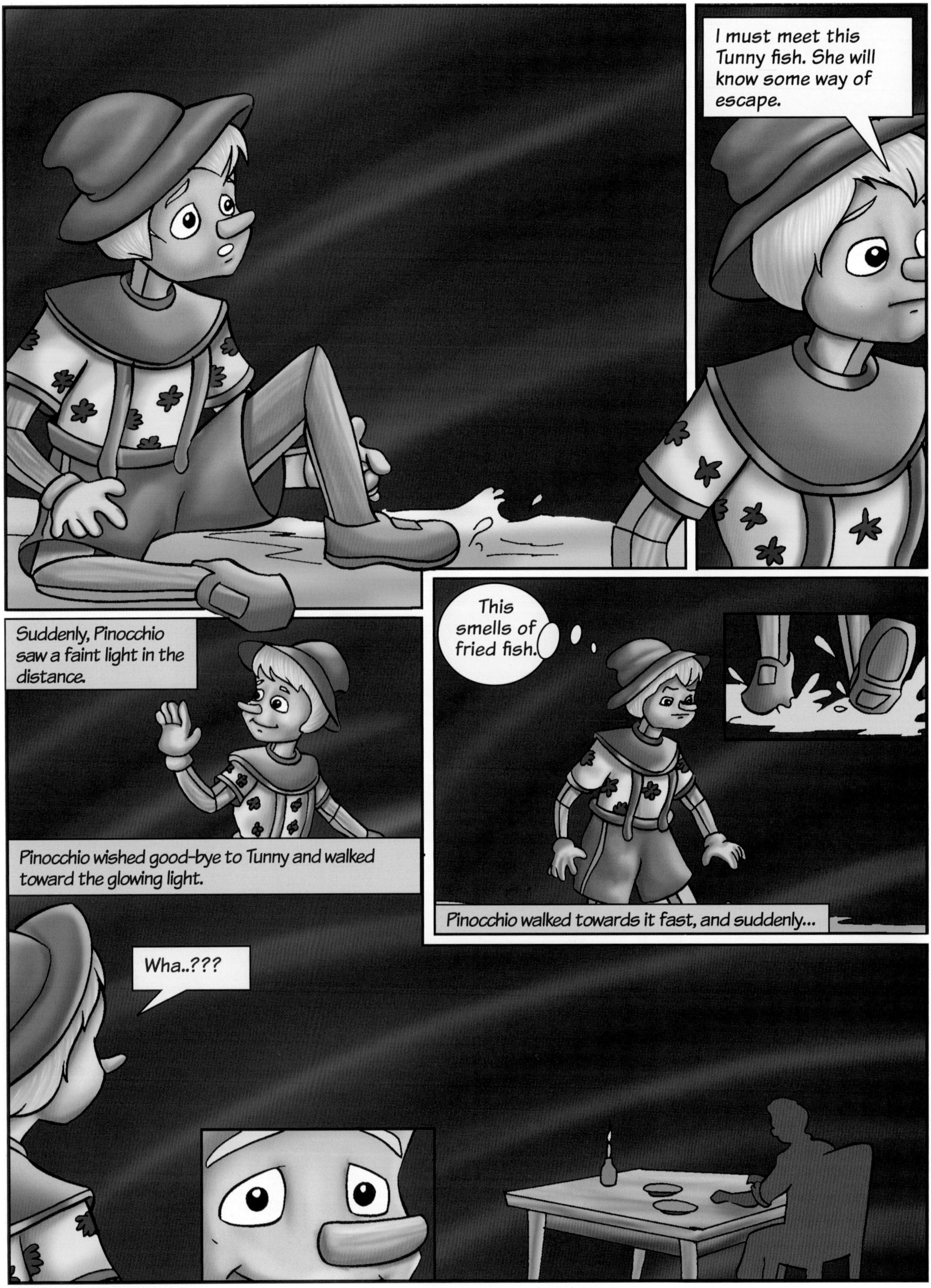
I must meet this Tunny fish. She will know some way of escape.
Suddenly, Pinocchio saw a faint light in the distance.
Pinocchio wished good-bye to Tunny and walked toward the glowing light.
This smells of fried fish.
Pinocchio walked towards it fast, and suddenly...
Wha..???

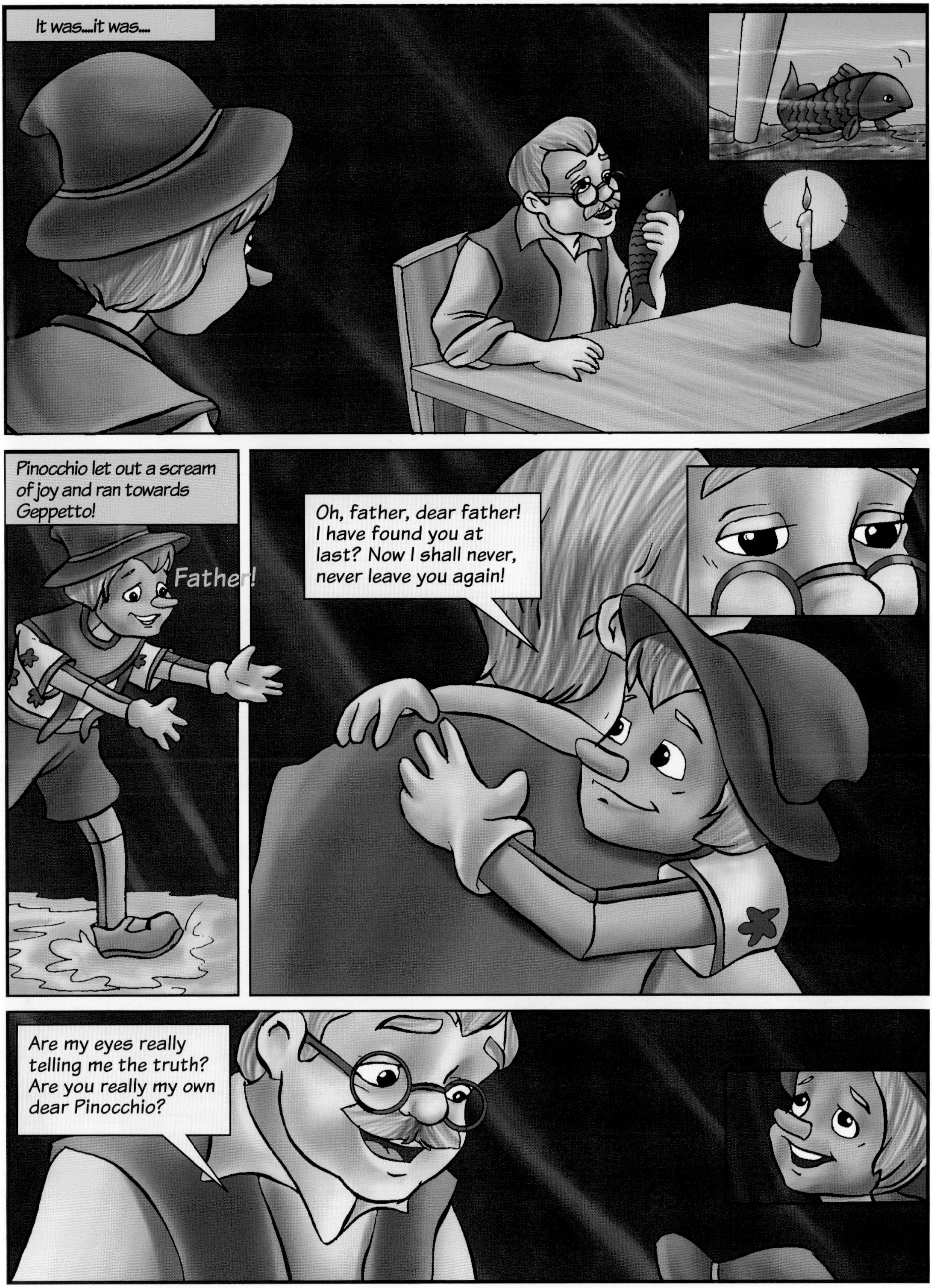
It was....it was....
Pinocchio let out a scream of joy and ran towards Geppetto!
Father!
Oh, father, dear father! I have found you at last? Now I shall never, never leave you again!
Are my eyes really telling me the truth? Are you really my own dear Pinocchio?

Pinocchio told Geppetto all, till his father's boat had disappeared among the waves.

From that day, my Pinocchio, I am living here. Today the last crumb is eaten and this candle you see here is the last one.

The Shark had also swallowed a ship full of provisions which had sustained Geppetto for two years.

Then, my dear father, there is no time to lose. We must try to escape.

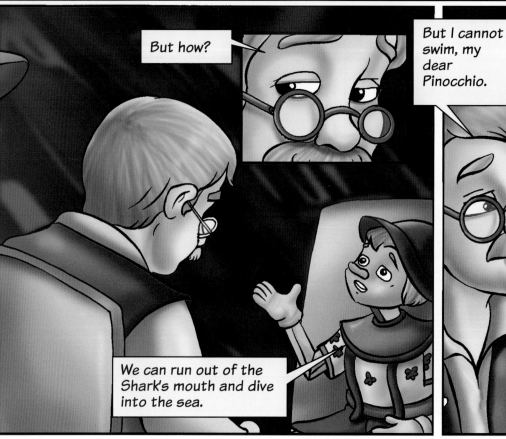

But how?

But I cannot swim, my dear Pinocchio.

We can run out of the Shark's mouth and dive into the sea.

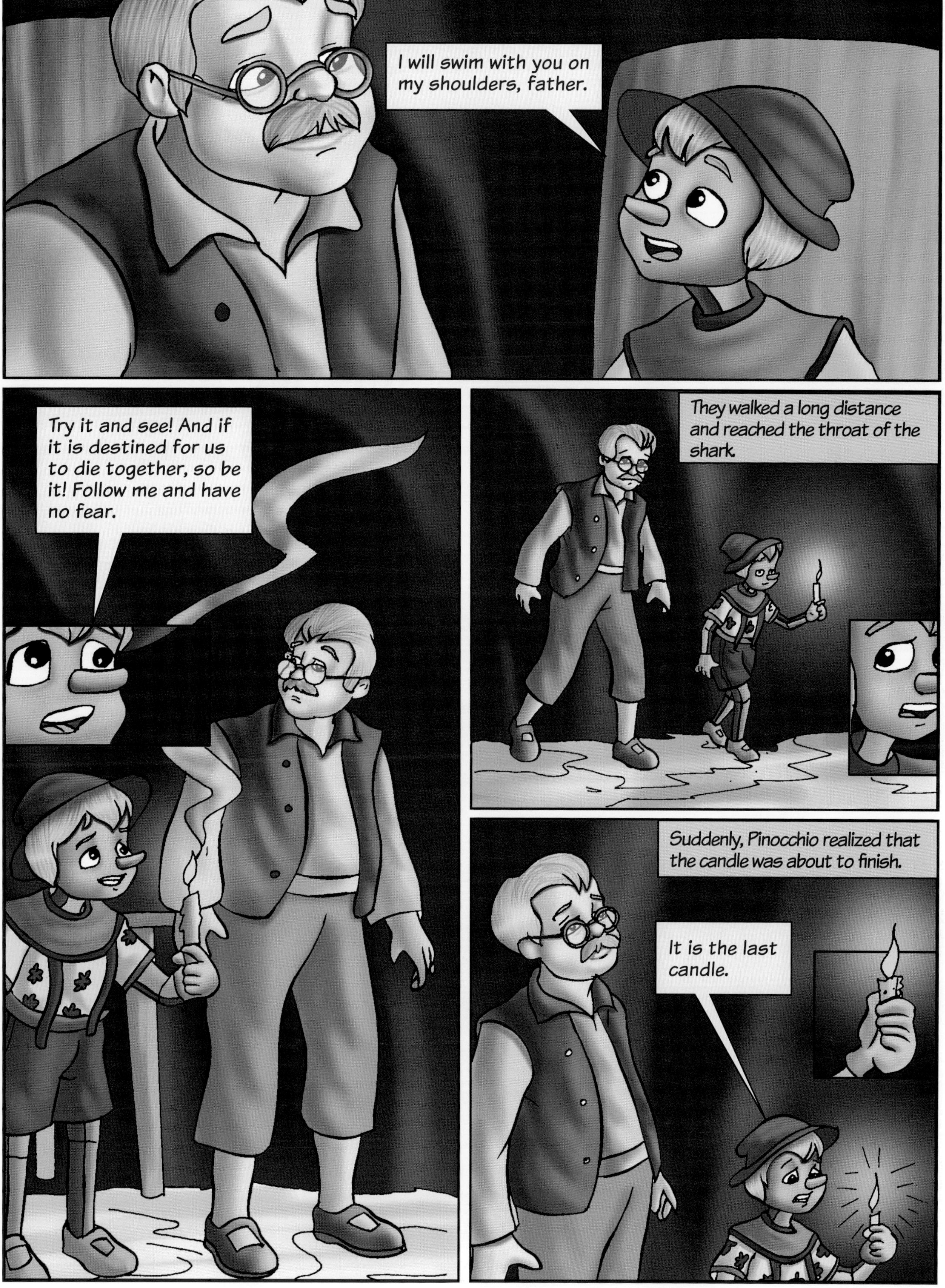
I will swim with you on my shoulders, father.
Try it and see! And if it is destined for us to die together, so be it! Follow me and have no fear.
They walked a long distance and reached the throat of the shark.
Suddenly, Pinocchio realized that the candle was about to finish.
It is the last candle.

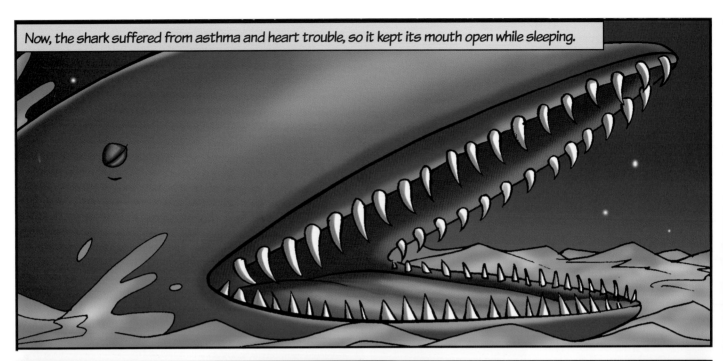

Now, the shark suffered from asthma and heart trouble, so it kept its mouth open while sleeping.

The Shark is fast asleep and we can escape. The sea is calm and the night is bright.
Follow me closely, Father.

AAAAAA.......

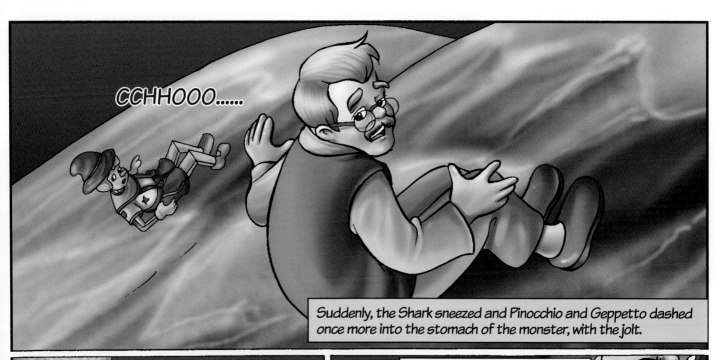

CCHHOOO......

Suddenly, the Shark sneezed and Pinocchio and Geppetto dashed once more into the stomach of the monster, with the jolt.

Now we are lost.

Why lost? Give me your hand, dear father. We must try again. Come with me and don't be afraid.

They climbed the shark's throat again and crossed its tongue.

Father, hold on tightly to my neck. I'll take care of everything else.

Splash!

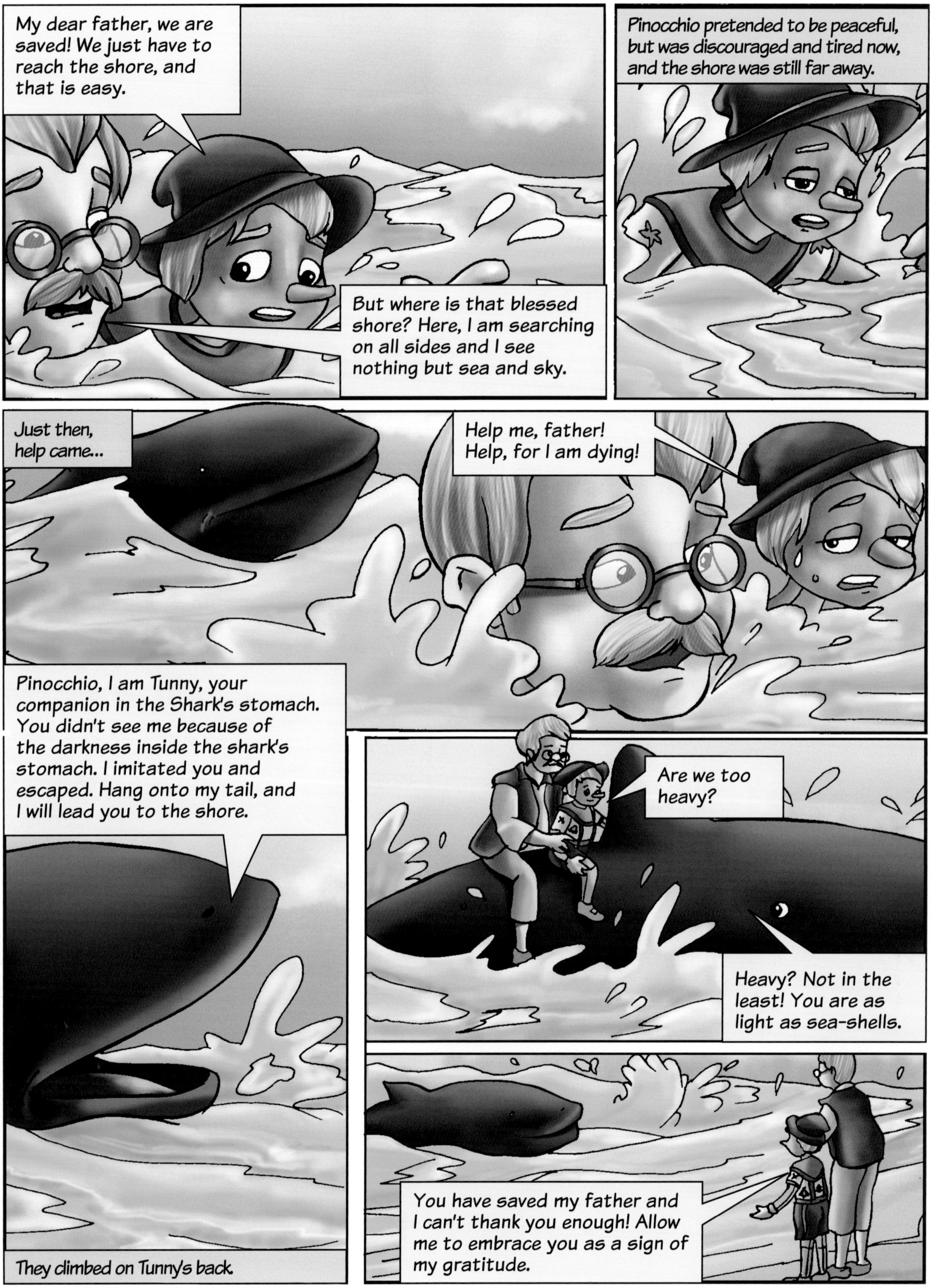
My dear father, we are saved! We just have to reach the shore, and that is easy.
But where is that blessed shore? Here, I am searching on all sides and I see nothing but sea and sky.
Pinocchio pretended to be peaceful, but was discouraged and tired now, and the shore was still far away.
Just then, help came...
Help me, father! Help, for I am dying!
Pinocchio, I am Tunny, your companion in the Shark's stomach. You didn't see me because of the darkness inside the shark's stomach. I imitated you and escaped. Hang onto my tail, and I will lead you to the shore.
They climbed on Tunny's back.
Are we too heavy?
Heavy? Not in the least! You are as light as sea-shells.
You have saved my father and I can't thank you enough! Allow me to embrace you as a sign of my gratitude.

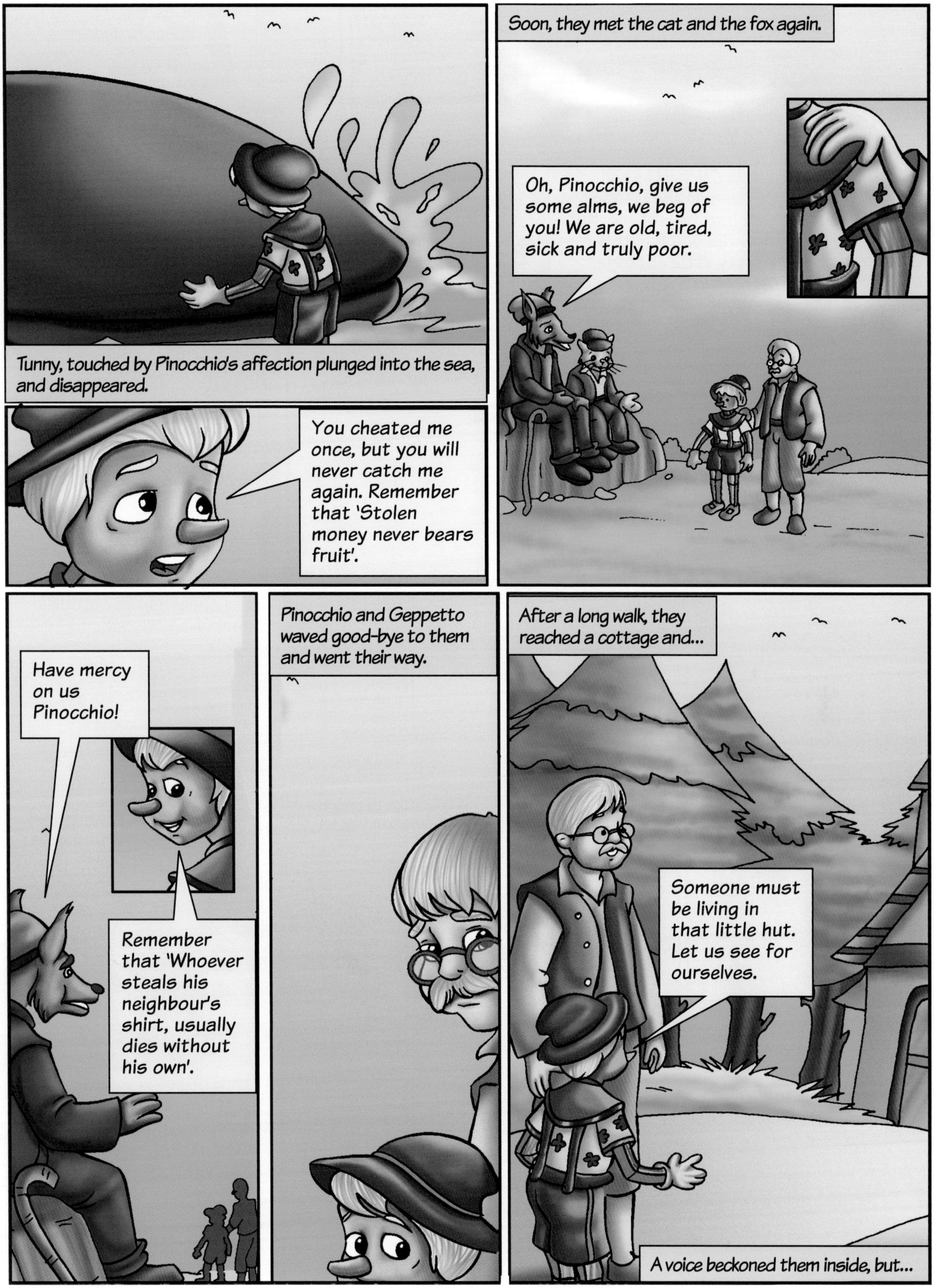
Tunny, touched by Pinocchio's affection plunged into the sea, and disappeared.
Soon, they met the cat and the fox again.
Oh, Pinocchio, give us some alms, we beg of you! We are old, tired, sick and truly poor.
You cheated me once, but you will never catch me again. Remember that 'Stolen money never bears fruit'.
Have mercy on us Pinocchio!
Remember that 'Whoever steals his neighbour's shirt, usually dies without his own'.
Pinocchio and Geppetto waved good-bye to them and went their way.
After a long walk, they reached a cottage and...
Someone must be living in that little hut. Let us see for ourselves.
A voice beckoned them inside, but...

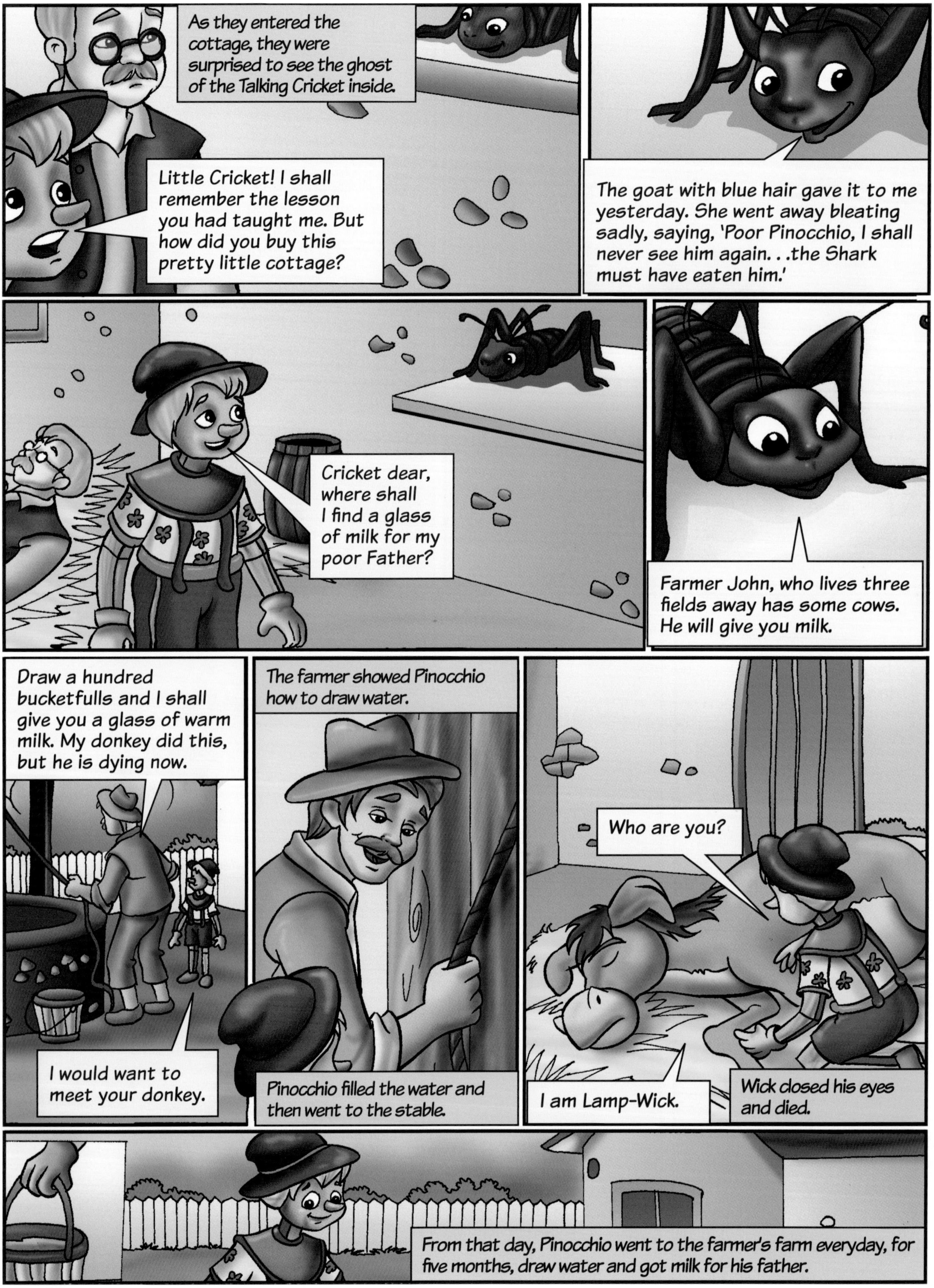
As they entered the cottage, they were surprised to see the ghost of the Talking Cricket inside.
Little Cricket! I shall remember the lesson you had taught me. But how did you buy this pretty little cottage?
The goat with blue hair gave it to me yesterday. She went away bleating sadly, saying, 'Poor Pinocchio, I shall never see him again. . .the Shark must have eaten him.'
Cricket dear, where shall I find a glass of milk for my poor Father?
Farmer John, who lives three fields away has some cows. He will give you milk.
Draw a hundred bucketfulls and I shall give you a glass of warm milk. My donkey did this, but he is dying now.
I would want to meet your donkey.
The farmer showed Pinocchio how to draw water.
Pinocchio filled the water and then went to the stable.
Who are you?
I am Lamp-Wick.
Wick closed his eyes and died.
From that day, Pinocchio went to the farmer's farm everyday, for five months, drew water and got milk for his father.

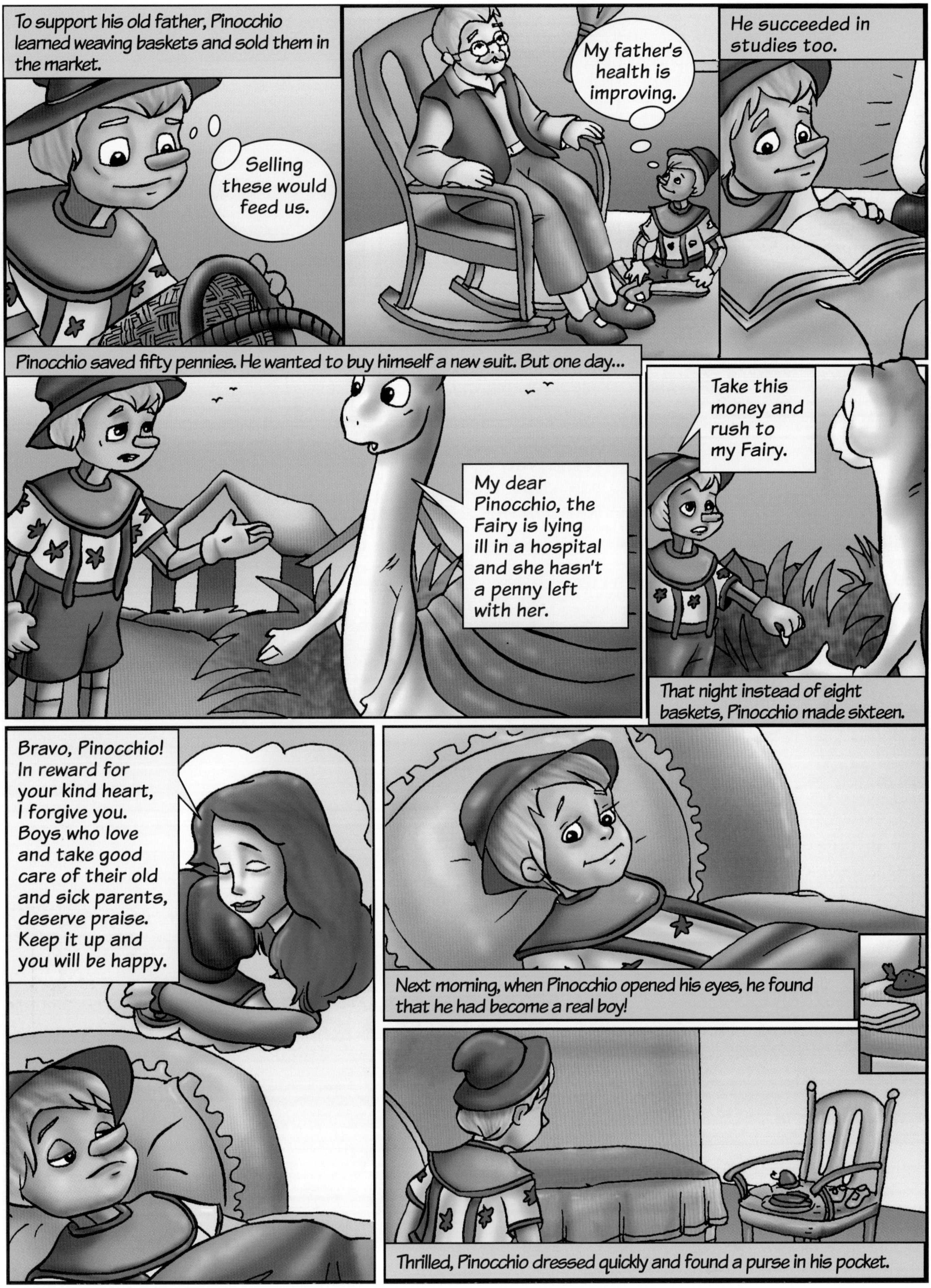
To support his old father, Pinocchio learned weaving baskets and sold them in the market.
Selling these would feed us.
My father's health is improving.
He succeeded in studies too.
Pinocchio saved fifty pennies. He wanted to buy himself a new suit. But one day...
My dear Pinocchio, the Fairy is lying ill in a hospital and she hasn't a penny left with her.
Take this money and rush to my Fairy.
That night instead of eight baskets, Pinocchio made sixteen.
Bravo, Pinocchio! In reward for your kind heart, I forgive you. Boys who love and take good care of their old and sick parents, deserve praise. Keep it up and you will be happy.
Next morning, when Pinocchio opened his eyes, he found that he had become a real boy!
Thrilled, Pinocchio dressed quickly and found a purse in his pocket.

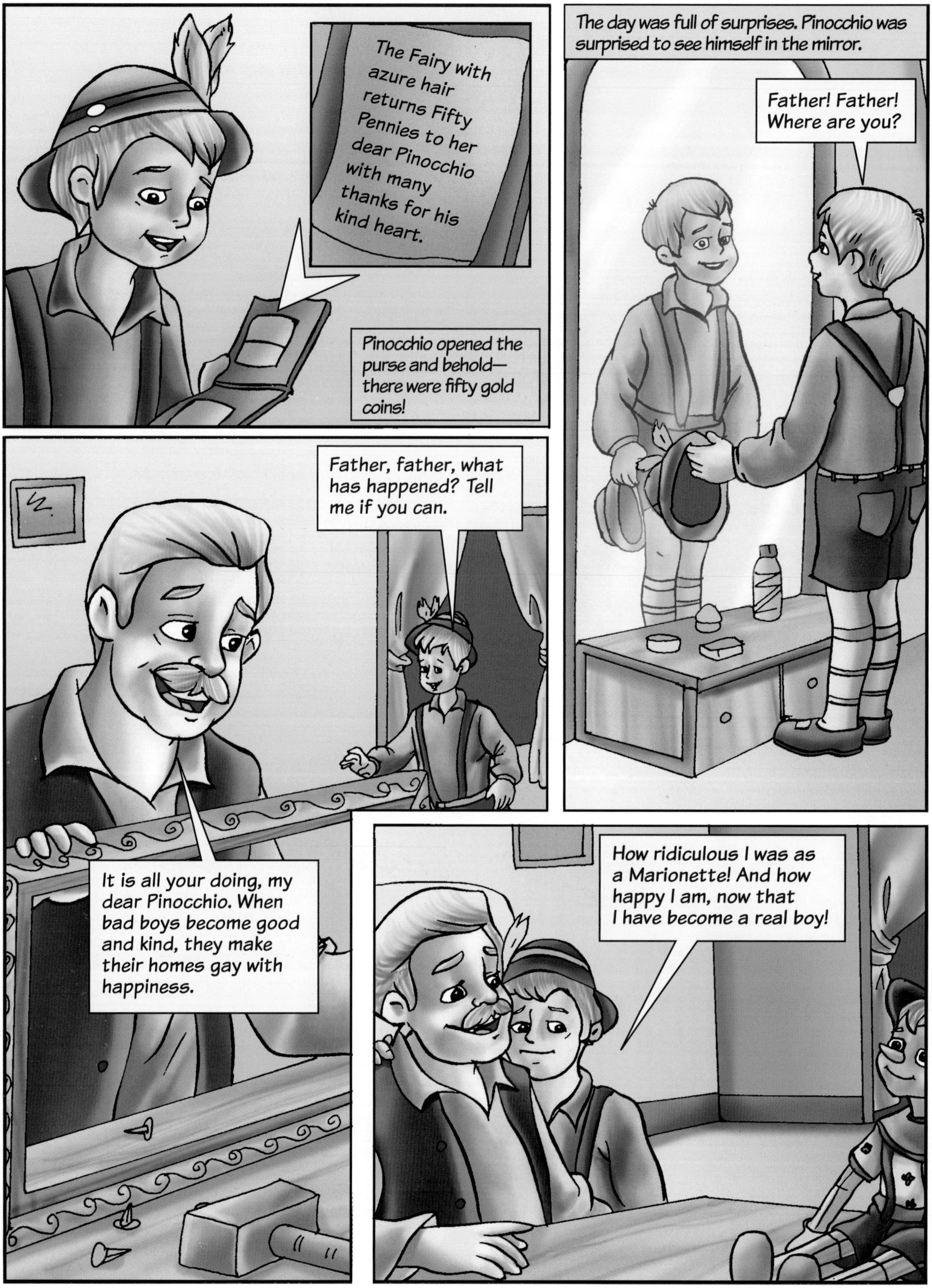
The Fairy with azure hair returns Fifty Pennies to her dear Pinocchio with many thanks for his kind heart.
Pinocchio opened the purse and behold—there were fifty gold coins!
The day was full of surprises. Pinocchio was surprised to see himself in the mirror.
Father! Father! Where are you?
Father, father, what has happened? Tell me if you can.
It is all your doing, my dear Pinocchio. When bad boys become good and kind, they make their homes gay with happiness.
How ridiculous I was as a Marionette! And how happy I am, now that I have become a real boy!